More praise for *Palmerino*

"Enthralling . . . An intriguing introduction to Violet Paget, and an unusual look into the mysteries of writing." —*Booklist*

"A supernaturally infused, innovative story . . . Pritchard's fertile imagination and presentation give new meaning to the expression 'a meeting of the minds.'" —*Kirkus Reviews*

"Fiction can reimagine flesh-and-blood folks to stunning effect . . . What a pleasure, then, to discover Melissa Pritchard's *Palmerino*, which envisions the life of Vernon Lee, the pen name and male persona of Englishwoman Violet Paget. Opening with the contemporary story of Sylvia, who discovers Lee while working at Villa il Palmerino in the Italian countryside and becomes her biographer, this work is related in sun-on-raindrops prose that draws in readers." —BARBARA HOFFERT, *Library Journal*

"At the heart of *Palmerino* lies beauty, grace, longing, love. Melissa Pritchard's picturesque prose is fertile, sensuous, a voice of insight, truth. Unique and refreshing as 'the great female soul that is Palmerino.' Gorgeous and heartbreaking. This book is a sensual treasure." —KIM CHINQUEE, author of *Pretty*

"Bounding between Italy today and of a century ago, a breathtaking gallop through intellectualism, feminism, sexuality, cultural history, honeysuckle, focaccia, plums, language, landscape, love, the supernatural, metafiction, mortality and resurrection, with Pritchard always firmly at the reins." —ANNE KORKEAKIVI, author of *An Unexpected Guest*

"A taut and elegant imagining of Vernon Lee's life that sparkles with *Einfühlung* for the writer, for Italy and for the love—wild, unconsummated, shattered—that lies at the heart of the best creative work. Weaving fact and fiction, past and present, *Palmerino* becomes its own beautiful mirror, a work that 'slips free of the self' to reveal the mysterious other. Sublime and moving, its gorgeous prose haunts the reader long after the last page." —ANA MENÉNDEZ, author of *Adios, Happy Homeland!*

"Seduction is at the lush heart of *Palmerino*. The Florentine retreat seduces us just as surely as it seduces the lonely and abandoned Sylvia, an historical novelist who in turn is seduced by the spirit of the brilliant Violet Paget, who lived there a century earlier. Writing as Vernon Lee, Violet's own seduction is one of the most quietly erotic scenes ever written." —PAMELA PAINTER, author of *Wouldn't You Like to Know*

"A brilliant novel whose cast of characters, strong, strange, vivid, eccentric, will make you feel enriched and enlivened, and will leave you wanting to visit, or to visit again, the rich interiors of Tuscany past and present, the opulent mysteries of its food and wine, and not least the magic of its natural landscapes and seasons." —C.K. STEAD, author of *Mansfield*

"In her subtle yet breathtaking new novel, *Palmerino,* Melissa Pritchard seduces us once again with her characteristically sensual and deeply poetic prose. Elegantly braiding time, this woven narrative is calibrated by Pritchard's exquisite erotic reckonings and resonant aesthetic reflections. In resurrecting Violet Paget/ Vernon Lee at our own historical moment (and by invoking a gallery of beloved and provocative artists and esthetes), Melissa Pritchard has provided for her readers a portrait-mirror in which to gaze—a glorious vision of both Palmerino and of a writer in pursuit of its history—one that would make even Oscar Wilde blush with envy." —DAVID ST. JOHN, author of *The Auroras*

"Melissa Pritchard stands out among contemporary writers for her ability to portray the complex inner lives of her characters. As we follow them through their experiences and memories into their dreams, we're invited to flex our own imaginations, even, if we're willing, to become more supple thinkers, thanks to this writer's supple prose."
—JOANNA SCOTT, author of *Follow Me*

Praise for Melissa Pritchard

"A writer at the height of her powers." —Oprah.com

"Dreamy and delightful."—NPR, *All Things Considered*

"Wildly imaginative . . . Endearingly quirky." —*Glamour*

"Precise and lucid." —*New York Times Book Review*

"The singularity of [Pritchard's] narrators remains indelible [and] shows that fiction still has the ability to shock and surprise." —*Washington Post*

"Melissa Pritchard has her GPS set to find the *how it is*—out there and in the heart." —SVEN BIRKERTS, author of *The Gutenberg Elegies: The Fate of Reading in an Electronic Age* and editor of *AGNI*

"Melissa Pritchard is one of our finest writers." —ANNIE DILLARD, author of *The Maytrees*

"I have admired Melissa Pritchard's writing for several years now for its wisdom, its humble elegance, and its earthy comedy." —RICK MOODY, author of *The Four Fingers of Death*

"Melissa Pritchard is a treasure." —BRADFORD MORROW, author of *The Diviner's Tale*

"Vivid, bold, and wickedly witty." —SENA JETER NASLUND, author of *The Fountain of St. James Court; or, Portrait of the Artist as an Old Woman*

"Melissa Pritchard's prose, that darkly lyrical firmament, is brightened by the dizzy luminous arrangement of her stars and satellites, her great gifts to us: humor, irony, kindness, brilliance." —ANTONYA NELSON, author of *Bound*

"Melissa Pritchard is a writer of immense talent." —PETER STRAUB, author of *A Dark Matter*

PALMERINO

PALMERINO

MELISSA PRITCHARD

BELLEVUE LITERARY PRESS
New York

First Published in the United States in 2014 by
Bellevue Literary Press, New York

For Information, Contact:
Bellevue Literary Press
NYU School of Medicine
550 First Avenue
OBV A612
New York, NY 10016

Palmerino is a work of fiction. References to real people, events, establishments,
organizations, or locales are intended only to provide a sense of authenticity, and
are used fictitiously. All other characters, incidents and places are products of the
author's imagination and are not to be construed as real.

Library of Congress Cataloging-in-Publication Data
Pritchard, Melissa.
    Palmerino / Melissa Pritchard.
        pages cm
    ISBN 978-1-934137-68-0 (alk. paper)
    1. Women authors—fiction. 2. Authors--Fiction. I. Title.
    PS3566.R578P36 2014
    813'.54—dc23

                                            2013035134

Bellevue Literary Press would like to thank all its generous
donors—individuals and foundations—for their support.

This publication is made possible by grants from:

  The National Endowment for the Arts

The New York State Council on the Arts with
the support of Governor Andrew Cuomo and
the New York State Legislature

and Amazon.com

Book design and composition by Mulberry Tree Press, Inc.
Manufactured in the United States of America.
first edition

1   3   5   7   9   8   6   4   2

ISBN 978-1-934137-68-0

For Mario Materassi, Federica Parretti, and Stefano Vincieri

with gratitude and love

Eros the melter of limbs (now again) stirs me—

sweetbitter unmanageable creature who steals in

If Not,
Winter
Fragments of Sappho
—Anne Carson

PALMERINO

Sylvia

A<small>N OLD-FASHIONED BLACK UMBRELLA</small>, half its ribs sprung, blocks the door leading down a stone staircase. The caretaker had held it over Sylvia's head as he'd walked her to the villa's entrance, used it, too, to carry in her luggage. From her bed this morning, it looks like some monstrous dark-wilted tulip.

Inside the taxi last evening, as the car had wound its way up narrow curves to Villa il Palmerino's twin gates, each crowned with an iron fleur-de-lis, she'd caught watery glimpses of villas hidden within drenched groves of palm, ilex, oak, and magnolia, of low stone walls shrouded with honeysuckle, each flower a star, orange splashed bright at its heart. It has been raining ever since, a soft downpour, cooling, telluric, fine-grained.

They had stayed in Palmerino's front villa last June, in a refurbished ground-floor apartment. But five months ago, the day after his sixtieth birthday, her husband, Philip, left her for his Russian colleague. Attempting a brave show—after all, hadn't his affair with Ivan been smoldering on and off for years?—Sylvia wrote to see if one of the other apartments in the front villa (definitely not that one) might be available for the month of June. Sorry, came Natalia Alberini's reply. All three apartments in the front villa were booked. However, if she liked (and yes, of course Natalia remembered her, *con piacere!*) she could have the large upstairs bedroom in her aunt's villa, near the back of the property, and for a reasonable rate, since Giustina would be away at an ashram in India. Natalia added she was delighted to hear that Sylvia was working on a novel inspired by Vernon Lee, the British Victorian writer who had lived at Villa il Palmerino. Glad their conversations last summer had resulted in this wonderful project. Terribly sorry, too, to hear of Sylvia's recent divorce. *Mi dispiace.*

For fifteen years, compensation, perhaps, for her marriage, Sylvia had enjoyed modest success as a novelist. Every other year (a broody hen laying her eggs, Philip had joked), she had produced a meticulously researched, conventionally written historical novel. The first books had sold surprisingly well, with Sylvia gathering a readership, mostly women. A few had written fan letters; on occasion, she answered. But the last two novels, one a romance set during the Albigensian Crusade in thirteenth-century France, the other a convoluted saga of rivalrous families during England's War of the Roses, had suffered dismal sales and been so negligibly reviewed that her New York agent, poised to retire from an industry he had turned intractably glum about, made it clear that Sylvia's next book needed to be far more appealing—"juicy," he'd actually said; less "plodding," he'd bluntly added—to even begin to slip Sylvia back into a semiprofitable stream of sales. Otherwise, she would find

herself, like so many mid-list authors, obsolete—minus a
publisher, minus readers and, worst of all, with no income.
His unsparing pronouncement had sent a whip of anxiety
through Sylvia's preparations for her trip. Aside from neatly
organized research materials, she'd packed haphazardly,
forgotten her raincoat, walking shoes, address book, forgotten a number of things.

This morning, the caretaker's sad, broken umbrella
seems to underscore the reality that Philip is in Paris on a
kind of honeymoon with his chalk-faced, garrulous lover,
while Sylvia is here, still in shock over her solitary existence. Even yesterday, in Rome, she'd received news that
Florentine friends she had counted on seeing were away—
both Alessandra and Valeria on holiday in Sardinia with
their husbands and children, and Cesare Lumachelli, an
old writing associate, in London with his English wife,
tending to his mother-in-law, who was ill and probably
dying. Cut off from Italian acquaintances, friendships she
had hoped to renew on her own, waking up in a stranger's
bedroom, Sylvia feels herself drifting near some precipice
of panic. How does one start over at fifty-six? Even the
luxury hotel she and Philip had always enjoyed in Rome,
steps from the Villa Borghese gardens, had felt preten-
tious, its luxury shameless. After one sleepless night in
the blindingly white chandeliered room with its cavernous dark green marble bathroom, she'd checked out, found
a small boutique hotel overlooking Piazza Cairoli, where
she could at least sit down and eat breakfast at a common
table with other travelers, like the shy English widower,
Robert, whose stammering attempts at conversation kept

circling back to the inexhaustible virtues of his dead wife, Margaret, or the pleasant Canadian couple who had raised four daughters (each neatly wed, each producing adorable grandchildren on schedule) and now, with complacency, were bent on seeing the world via cruises and guidebooks, "while we still can."

Sylvia and Philip had had no children, the reason for their lackluster sex life, in hindsight, bitterly evident. Without siblings, she had nursed her invalid father until he died three years ago; her mother, long afflicted by dementia, followed less than a year later. Now there was no one with any long history of knowing or genuinely loving her. With both her parents dead, without Philip's familiar, if chilly, presence, there is only a terrifying, almost trite silence, pointing, it would seem, to eternity.

Naked, Sylvia crosses to one of the windows, unlatches and opens the dark green louvered shutters onto a postcard-perfect view of vineyards edged with the satiny vermillion bloom of poppies. The early morning air is cool; she crosses her arms over her breasts, feels more than physically weary from the overseas flight. What she feels is unanchored. Peripheral. A bit pointless.

V.

———⊗⊗⊗———

She arrived late last night, bringing the damage of too much rain. Fell asleep in a bed quilted with copies of old letters, photographs, Italian vocabularies, a train ticket from Rome.

This morning, the rooster digs talons into his rough pulpit of kindling and crows, raspy, halfhearted. Palma, the German shepherd, skulks past the kitchen garden, vulpine, only a little cunning left in her. In the distance, deep within the stone tower of San Martino, an iron bell tolls.

Folding back the green shutters of an upstairs window, she appears within its frame, auburn hair, lilac pale shoulders.

One of Sargent's earliest portraits.

Or a white rose, dried to dust between the pages of a story, its ending unfinished, until now.

Sylvia

———— ∞ ————

Loosely knotting the sash of her apple green silk robe, Sylvia furls the shabby umbrella, props it against the wall before making her way, barefoot, down the cool stone staircase and through the dining room to a small galleylike kitchen. Waiting for the little Italian coffeemaker to boil on its ring of sputtering blue-and-gold flame, she hears television noise from a room off the dining room, sports, a soccer match. Giustina's upstairs bedroom has a television, as well. Heavy, outdated, it sits angled on a bureau, inches from the bed. All last night, it had made periodic clicking and hissing noises, as if attempting to turn itself off and on. Just before sunrise, wakened by the sounds, Sylvia had sat up, to see the screen glowing lunar silver before it faded to mauve, then black.

In the kitchen, strung from the kitchen's low, beamed ceiling are dusty bundles of dried herbs, ropes of pearly garlic, their white-rumped bulbs sere, brittle. Above the granite sink, messily stacked with unwashed dishes, an iron-barred window overlooks a bright length of lawn bordered by orange and yellow daylilies, the smooth green incline interrupted by a cluster of sapling olive trees. At the slope's summit, a rope clothesline sags, grins with rain-sodden clothing, while just beyond, plum dark clouds are moving in, threatening rain. A sudden rogue gust of wind buffets the young olive trees, followed by a short crash of thunder just above her head. A rooster crows nearby; then a sharp spit of rain strikes against the window.

Sylvia's idea to work mornings, then take the local bus into Florence, spend afternoons wandering through churches, galleries, and museums seems untenable, today at least. She doubts the caretaker's dilapidated umbrella would survive a single excursion, and she has forgotten her own. Heading back upstairs with her coffee, she notices a crack running the length of one of the dining room's white plaster walls, a dried taupe swag of grapevine tacked all along it, curious camouflage, calling attention to the defect. If she is about to be confined by rain, she thinks, she may as well review her research notes, skim through her two dog-eared biographies of Vernon Lee, rearrange her collection of scanned archival photos. A wet, dreary day could at least prove productive.

Stepping over a gray cat asleep on a middle stair, she stops a moment in front of a wooden niche on the tiny landing, studies the Christ carved of blond-grained wood, sinuous against its thin cross of ebony. Notices a calendar of Hindu saints in stark, garish colors, propped against the nailed feet.

Sylvia and Philip had briefly met Giustina, Natalia's aunt, the summer before. A tall woman with a distracted, apologetic air, a devotee of Swami Sivananda, Giustina traveled twice a year to her guru's ashram in Kerala, and shared her home with the caretaker, Remo, who labored dutifully, if inconsistently, over tasks large and small, providing him a narrow ledge in the world. Inside her home, original servants' quarters for another, more formal villa concealed nearby behind black spires of cypress and a maze of footpaths, Remo moves soundlessly. In the days to come, Sylvia will never know where or when she will come upon the caretaker, his pugilist's torso and short, bowed legs, his head bald except for a gray curlicue of hair, vestigial, at the nape of his deeply creased neck. And since his English and her Italian are equally execrable, their communications will prove brief, excruciatingly polite. With smiles resembling forced grimaces, they will take mutual refuge from awkward attempts at conversation by stroking the feral cats that live everywhere, roaming the kitchen's marble countertops, napping on the big rustic dining table or on the plain stone staircase to Sylvia's room. Remo, feline himself, sleeps curled on a short blue couch off the front room, his television always on, its sound turned low, broadcasting the forced, hysteric vitality of Italian game shows, melodramas, soccer matches.

Upstairs, Sylvia stands quite still in the middle of another woman's bedroom. Pristine at its center, the room grows increasingly cluttered at its edges yet still gives, overall, an impression of austerity. A bed, two plain desks, an antique bureau, a dozen or so shelves filled with pale blue subscription journals—the teachings of Swami Satyananda Saraswati—Hindi and English translations arranged neatly by month and year. The floor of Giustina's bedroom is ocher brick, the walls white, with two unscreened green-shuttered windows. The ceiling is whitewashed, evenly striped with rough-hewn beams. From the west window, the view is of a vineyard and vegetable garden, from the south, the scene directly beneath is of a flagstone veranda shaded by a pergola of entangled honeysuckle and trumpet vine. Branches of an enormous *tiglio,* or lime tree, grow close to the open window, as if wanting to reach deep into the room with long, mottled gray arms. Sylvia imagines herself a sparrow concealed inside the *tiglio,* nesting in its fragrant, sun-ribboned green nest. In the drone of honeybees from the tree's topmost, blooming branches, she will discover a golden daylong sound, a marvelous aural industry; she already knows that the tree's unshowy golden-white blossoms, brewed as a tisane, are known to calm the nerves, induce sleep. From Giustina's double bed, Sylvia has a generous view of this tree. The bed itself is simple, its headboard upholstered in embroidered heavy white linen. Draped along it are ashram shawls and scarves of marigold and blood orange, sacred *malas,* or necklaces, made from the brown seeds of India's *rudraksha* tree, holy to Shiva, believed to confer blessings.

On two walls of the room, randomly hung oil paintings crowd against one another. Most are framed; all are signed by Giustina's late father, Paolo Alberini, a well-known Florentine artist and copyist. Time-darkened portraits of Madonnas with upturned, limpid gazes. A naked female saint, her body plump, eluctable, trussed with rope, bloodlessly pierced with arrows. Gilt framed portraits of eighteenth-century ladies with composed, faintly recriminatory expressions. A modern-looking nude with dark cropped hair, her thick green-daubed flesh pressing, as if protesting, against the confinement of an antique gold leaf frame. Here and there among the paintings, casually thumb-tacked, are cheap color posters of Pope Giovanni Paolo II (*Non abbiate paura*) 1920–2005, of Mother Teresa, of Swami Sivananda. Wedged randomly among these are old black-and-white photos, each in a black frame—members of the Alberini family, grandparents, brothers, sisters, aunts, uncles, children, posed in groups outside villas, beside the sea, on bicycles, or gathered, feasting, around a large table. Hindu holy calendars hang, too, from the walls, time stopped and squared at an expired month, an expired year. The room feels indifferent to time; no steadying sequence of weeks or years, no roundness or linearity—the effect on Sylvia is consoling, almost freeing.

The windows, louvered shutters open to the cool air, the rain striking unevenly on the two pergolas, one out-side the kitchen, dense with grapevine, the other with its honeysuckle and trumpet vine, the mingled perfume of rain, honeysuckle, and lime—all make Sylvia drowsy. She stands barefoot, sipping the black, almost syrupy coffee, her gaze soft, lost among Palmerino's soaked, half-wild gardens, the rounded, benign hills, dark umber and gold in the distance. Even though Remo is downstairs, forced in by weather, she feels, for a moment, alone. Like the only creature left in the world.

In the early afternoon, when the skies clear to an enam-eled blue and the sun is clean and hot, Sylvia goes outside to wander the lush, almost steaming property. Stepping out from the villa, she comes upon three cats threading in and out of a cavelike shelter of overgrown shrubbery. One, a rangy, skeletal tomcat, writhes voluptuously, almost indecently, against a rinsed gravel footpath. A short walk up the path takes her beyond the vineyards and vegetable garden, where she finds, inside a rain-pooled pasture, a roan mare up to her hocks in purplish mud, cropping grass beneath the shade of wild plum trees.

All around the villa and its property, birds dart between untrimmed hedgerows of laurel and boxwood, vanish into overarching canopies of deciduous trees, oak, maple, magnolia, pine. Along the main path, just wide enough for a small car, low shrubs of rosemary, silver lavender, and peppermint give off a mixed odor, resinous, powdery sweet, while evenly spaced along the edges of the rain-blackened flagstone veranda are dwarf lemon trees in terra-cotta pots, intensely yellow orblike fruits gleaming among polished green ovate leaves. And set on window ledges, old chairs and wooden benches, on the flagstones themselves, blooming in profuse bursts of summer color, are pots of scarlet-belled, violet-skirted fuchsia, papery pink and orange bougainvillea, dense, fluffy heads of grayish blue hydrangea, lipstick pink geranium, and one tall staked clematis vine with starlike severe purple flowers. Sheltered beneath the pergola, sunlight winking and glittering among the honeysuckle and trumpet vine, are two long tables, each covered with tan oilcloth, both oilcloths littered with fading *tiglio* blossoms, runelike gouts of birdlime, and tiny serpentine trails of ants. Hung along one white plaster wall of the villa are old garden tools—blunt and rusted scythes, hoes, rakes—and graying baskets bursting with sprays of dried brown or brittle white flowers. Standing against one of the loggia's wooden pillars is a crudely built open cupboard, four wooden shelves warped and bowed, crowded with quilted glass canning jars in tints of light topaz and sea green. Sealed inside each of these jars are fruits from Giustina Alberini's orchard, marmalades and jams, strangely hued, burnt orange, dark red, whitish green, pale brown, lilac-amber. The ink on handwritten labels pasted to each jar is faded to a pale sepia script—*fico, susina, arancia, rabarbaro*. Above the shelves hangs a large homemade photo collage, the images washed to ghastly blues, sad dilute oranges—blurred images of somber, skinny children lined up outside an orphanage somewhere in India. Directly beneath the rain- and sun-warped montage sits a wood box with a coin slot, a hand-printed sign taped to the box: *proceeds from the sale of the marmellata go to the children, dei bambini, of Sivananda Math.* Sylvia wonders how many coins have been dropped into the musty darkness of the homemade box. If the *marmellata* has yet turned to poison.

By dusk, it is raining again. Rain will fall steadily for three days and three nights, until the air is saturated with a verdant mossy tinge. When she does see him, Remo will only shrug a little and sigh before limping back to his television, which she hears like a vague dream of people in another room, talking. Forced into a solitude that holds twin bass notes of doubt and isolation, Sylvia begins to write, hesitant at first, then at a comforting, almost breakneck speed. The unrelenting downpour—nothing like this has been seen in thirty years, she thought she understood Remo to say—the watery spell under which she writes.

For three days, her room remains dark even at midday, the rough bedsheets and carnelian-colored blanket chilly and damp to the touch. And even with the swarm and hum of bees in the upper tiers of the lime tree silenced, the soporific, heady perfume of lime and honeysuckle still floods her senses.

For the first time in months, she feels a welcome, reckless absorption in her work. Instead of the weight of her previous books, too stiffly fortified, embalmed by facts, she decides to risk improvisation, spontaneous vignettes, a series of light sketches. On the second day, it occurs to Sylvia that beyond describing this woman's childhood, she intends to simplify, even bypass, much of her (turbulent) life and most of her (nearly forgotten) achievements. Instead, she is going to write about the two women Vernon Lee adored, abandon her old strategy—the methodical, conscientious, dull costuming of facts. Who knows, she might surprise her agent, might shock herself by the kind of story she will tell.

What she does know, as surely as if some invisible presence had whispered it in her ear, is that she has come to Villa il Palmerino, betrayed and alone, to write about love.

Violet Paget

Château Saint-Léonard
Boulogne-sur-Mer
France, 1856

What to make of this squalling infant, conceived by an English widow of means and a French tutor of vague aristocratic lineage? Of Violet Paget, half sister to Eugene Lee-Hamilton, eleven years older and already remote as a distant planet? What to make of this plain little prodigy, born a ruler's width from the schoolroom, her cradle a foursquare stack of eighteenth-century books, her mother's milk spurting Voltaire from one breast, dribbling Rousseau from the other? Fated to trail in her mother's restless, volatile wake, Violet's childhood will consist of traveling by horse-drawn carriage from one off-season watering hole to another—from Germany to France to Switzerland to Italy and all the lopsided way around again. Matilda Paget, who fled Britain because she "loathed the English Sunday," will shape her daughter's existence into one long, interminable English Sunday with regimented walks and monologues patched from her own follied, capricious mind. Matilda, who holds all men but her son in contempt, will school Violet herself, will mold this strange, unattractive creature into a formidable brain, a girl who, one day, will insist on dressing *comme un homme*.

Wiesbaden
Germany
December 1861

The schoolmaster's eldest daughter, her white blond braids entwined with scarlet ribbon, smells of cinnamon and sugar, of crushed clove and anise, of the *pfeffernüsse* cookies she has just baked with her mother and five sisters. It is nightfall, and Franziska squeezes her little charge's black-mittened hand in her own as they leave the marketplace, with its temporary forest of Christmas trees, resinous black-green firs, stiff and triangular as polished toys. When a sweep of snow sparkles down in the darkness, blowing at a fierce, cutting slant across the child's anxious face, Franziska laughs and says, "*Mein liebes Kind,* do not worry. It is only the miller and the baker, quarreling in heaven!"

Inside the Pagets' rented lodgings, Franziska hurries upstairs to lay a fire in the nursery, while in the candlelit foyer, five-year-old Violet presses one small, keen eye against the iron keyhole of her father's study, beholding a scene in the shape of that keyhole, a round, then tapering confusion of greenness, a longish white bit of her father's profile, his thin, pendulous nose, crow's wing of oiled hair, rapier tip of black mustache, spying as he stoops to twist a bit of glassy ornament onto her tree, *hers!*—cut down that morning by her father and shouldered out from the forest. Tomorrow night, Christmas Eve, her tree will blaze with lit wax tapers, casting a starry haze over the hard orange tangerines and burnished lady apples, the glass ornaments and white paper cones of sugared walnuts.

Sitting close to the nursery fire, sucking on her right thumb, always the right, Violet nests, mouselike, in Franziska's lap as her governess reads aloud from their favorite poem, Schiller's "The Child Murderess." Content, she breathes in Franziska's cinnamon pastry scent, pets the twin plaits of hair, faintly greasy ropes of white gold on which to climb into a land of spired castles, magic serpents, and wicked dragons. Franziska is the most comforting creature on earth, yet in April, she will abandon Violet to marry the local upholsterer, who, ever since he spotted her in church one Sunday, has besieged the schoolmaster's eldest, prettiest daughter with a blizzard of adoring letters, each more flowery than his most expensive satin fabric, each beginning the same: "My dearest little goldfish . . ."

Bernese Thun
Switzerland
December 1866

In the white schoolroom high above the Aar River, Violet's new Swiss governess, Fräulein Marie Schulpbach, warms herself beside the sky blue porcelain stove. She is baking two red apples and heating *café au lait* to pour into two blue-and-white bowls, while her pupil squeaks out dusty sums with a stub of chalk on a black slate. Only when Violet finishes her sums, her German conjugations, and her weekly letter in German to her brother, Eugene, away at Oxford ("Dearest *Bruder* . . . Love, Violette," accompanied by a pencil sketch of herself in a short ballet skirt, an envelope in one hand, a quill in the other), will Marie reward Violet by reading aloud from Goethe or even from one of the Grimms' fairy tales. In a succession of deeply silent, dark winter days, science, poetry, theory, and legend mix most wonderfully in both of their heads. Perched on Marie Schulpbach's knees, her legs in their itchy nut brown woolen tights dangling nearly to the floor, or settled in Marie's rustling black taffeta lap, Violet dreamily turns the pages of one of their thickly embossed orange-labeled books as Marie reads from Mozart's letters or Goethe's memoirs, his laureled profile on the cover, or from Violet's newest favorite, Joseph von Scheffel's *Der Trompeter von Säckingen*, a fantastical tale of roving musicians, a baron's clever daughter, and Hiddigeigei, the magical tomcat. Left mostly alone, Violet and Fräulein Marie Schulpbach float like cumulus clouds shot through with the gold of literature, memoirs, poetry, and fantasy, while outside their schoolroom, far below, the marbled green-and-white tumult of the Aar, glacial and aloof, rushes past.

Nice
France
December 1867

Near the end of another of their seaside walks along the Promenade des Anglais, with Matilda intoning from a fresh translation of Thomas Paine (the inward panorama of human liberty blinding her to physical sea and shore, to the stately rough-latticed pillars of Egyptian palms), they collide, literally, with their new neighbors, the FitzWilliam Sargents, an American couple with two children, John Singer, Violet's age, and his younger sister, Emily. And while Matilda sees nothing useful about walking beyond inflicting tendentious philosophies and lectures on the corruption of organized religion on her eleven-year-old daughter, Mrs. Sargent proves to be a free spirit, seeking out ever more fantastical sights, sublime sounds, dramatic, diverting histories. With Matilda's permission, she invites Violet, along with her own two children, to operas, the theater, museums, parks, and galleries, gives a revolutionary change of scenery to Violet's shut-up world of books and spartan walks. Delighted to describe herself as a high priestess of localities, Mrs. Sargent, an amateur watercolorist, introduces Violet to the classical Roman notion of genius loci, or spirit of place. And while her mother hardly comprehends such an adventuresome approach to existence, neither does she object to Violet's being placed, from time to time, in Mrs. Sargent's care.

In Nice, the French doors of the Pagets' ground-floor apartment open onto a drab garden edged by dwarf roses, which at Christmastime put forth a scentless carmine bloom. In this cramped space, Violet and John pass winter afternoons playing at morbid sets of charades. Today, for instance, Violet is not Violet, but Queen Elizabeth, and John is Robert, Earl of Essex, about to be decapitated for treason. Later, they may wander into the decrepit gardens of Villa Piol, search for wet, blackened figs fallen over the orchard walls, hidden in the long yellow grass.

Folding a maternal wing over this timid but precocious child, Mrs. Sargent draws Violet close, invites her to the family's weekly opera night, to their rented home for supper afterward, where John and Violet, stretched full length on the carpet, draw and paint before rolling over onto their backs, piping bits of libretti from Verdi or Donizetti, sweet tendrils of song rising, absorbed, lost, in the lavishly corniced pale pistachio ceiling

Villa Borghese
Rome
December 1868

In Rome now, Mrs. Paget's pedagogical walks resume. Every sunless afternoon on the cold, empty Pincian Hill bordering the Villa Borghese, Violet endures her mother's ambulatory education, a skewed rhetoric of world history, the postulates of Euclid, a bit of Racine, and, always, phrenology (the location of Causality being halfway between the brows and the ears, alongside Ideality and Veneration), teachings that conclude, unvaryingly, with a meager tea at their current lodgings on Piazza Mignanelli. Fortunately, the Sargents have taken up residence nearby, in a home at the top of the Spanish Steps near Trinità dei Monti. Every morning, twelve-year-old Violet waits for John to appear in his Eton pepper-and-salt jacket, dodging the usual gathering of beggars and artists' models, skipping down seven flights of the Spanish Steps, broad marble steps, their sallow gray-veined patterns flowing forever down, like frozen water.

Compared to the Swiss cleanliness of Thun, or the indulgent blue-gold light of Nice, with its fashionable lyre-backed chairs, Rome is a grim funerary procession. Filthy streets of slick wine-colored mud and stinging wild nettle, whole seasons of trash carelessly heaped over broken monuments and melancholic statuary, heavy plum and slate skies—Violet feels her every step, however light, sinking into yet another stranger's grave. That first winter in Rome horrifies her, the city a gloomy place littered and heavy with marble antiquities, starved horses in broken harnesses, nightmarish crevices of poverty gaping open at every turn. Rome is an endless cemetery, and except for her hours with John, she hates it.

Mornings, they slip into the Villa Borghese to wander the park's endless gardens and secret grottoes. When the old French-cursing warden catches them setting fire with a magnifying glass to the leathery dark leaves of a bay tree—*enfants mal élevés!*—they find fresh entertainment draping themselves over a wall of the Pincian terrace, pitching handfuls of acorns at the mud-spattered sea of grunting pigs huddled outside the Porta del Popolo.

And always there is the pleasure of sitting inside Nazzarri's cake shop on the Piazza di Spagna, reading novels, sipping from cups of hot chocolate so stiff and thick, they must stand their tall spoons upright, competing to see whose will topple first.

One winter morning in the Villa Borghese, near the Temple of Diana, splashing through a dry bronze surf of fallen leaves, they accidentally uncover, lying still against pungent dark soil mixed with pinkish stones, a dead sparrow.

The bird's body, flattened, perhaps beneath a horse's hoof, composed upon an oval bed of its own stomach contents— a small stain of crushed red pomegranate seed—is shocking and sacred. John touches a finger to the drab taupe feathers, still warm. They wonder at how recently the bird must have been winging its way through bay hedges and trees. Moved by the sparrow's fate, the children stand before La Fontana dei Cavalli Marini, the Fountain of Sea Horses, and each with a cold, chapped hand pressed against the other's heart, solemnly commit their lives, from that moment on, to Art—Violet as a writer, John an artist. Afterward, they take up running along the wide tops of stone walls, sliding down like swift, pale lizards, escaping the warden, who, somehow, is never far away—*enfants mal élevés!*—slipping down silver pathways, avenues of fierce black ilex, vanishing like sprites into the maple, oak, and cypress woods until, breathless, holding their sides, aching from laughter, they find themselves back on the broad gray Pincian, a street deserted and freezing, evenly marked by empty benches, flat as signature lines with no notes.

Hotel Molars
Via Gregoriana
Rome
1869

A clatter of iron-rimmed coach wheels on great square stones, tablets black and undulant as licorice, and now Violet, barefoot in her muslin nightgown, is awake, unlatching the wooden shutters. Leaning from a third-floor window overlooking Piazza Mignanelli, she sees a long line of papal coaches, each scarlet as a pomegranate, gilded and tasseled, drawn by white horses with red plumes. A scarlet-caped eminence steps down from each of the coaches, helped by lackeys in gold-trimmed livery, as a stream of *peni-tenti*, rising like oily black smoke from hell's crevices, mute wraiths from the filthiest, dankest corners of the piazza, from neighboring alleyways and streets, swarms forward. Wearing rough hoods with ragged holes for eyes and loose shrouds of scarlet or black, they shake their wooden alms boxes, the few paltry coins inside ringing out a common, piteous speech.

It is the first day of Advent, and from now until Christmas, Violet will be wakened each morning by a drone of bagpipes, the blaring of fifes, and the beating of drums in the piazza directly beneath her window. In neighboring butcher shops, long, fat sausages and squat hams garlanded with bay leaf and ribbon hang in rows, like rude rosy ornaments. The whole wintry, colorless place she knows as her neighborhood in Rome has been transformed overnight into glittering storybook scenes. Just before Christmas Day, Mrs. Sargent takes John, Emily, and Violet to Piazza Navona to view the gigantic Christmas crèche with its painted terracotta figures, then to the extravagant Christmas Fair near the Pantheon, at Piazza Sant'Eustachio, where each of them can buy, for only a few coins, tiny *pupazzi* and other little presents to give one another during the feast of Epiphany.

One morning, when it is still pitch-black out, freezing, before even the bagpipes, fifes, and drums can blare and beat beneath her window, Violet's mother shakes her from sleep and a servant hurriedly buttons her into strange, stiff black clothing, takes her downstairs, and bundles her into a two-seat cab. Crushed between her mother and the servant, quaking with cold, Violet eventually finds herself inside the Vatican. Kneeling beside Mrs. Paget, surrounded by hundreds of black-robed women with veiled faces, Violet gazes up into the wide gilt cupola as the first rays of the sun stream through the highest, smallest windows, illuminating the enormous gold letters: *Tu es Petrus.* The vastness of the cupola, the breaking light, the blue smoke of frankincense branching upward, the sober rows of black-shrouded women—are like a dream. And when a single note from an unseen trumpet splits the silence, Violet, on tiptoe in her drown of black cloth, glimpses above the steel bayonets of the papal guards an approaching undulation of white ostrich feathers with golden tassels—the papal procession, the swaying throne of Pius IX, the creamy columned folds of his pontifical robes. Otherworldly creatures, angels, fairies, djinns, spring forth from Violet's imagination, byzantine visions floating out from the cool, brassy throats of trumpets. Incense lingers, a pungent bluish smoke above the bowed, motionless rows of black-veiled women before dissipating, overtaken by the first gold rays of the sun.

After that Advent, that Christmas, Violet is entranced by all she had once despised about Rome—the cold mausoleums of galleries, the enigmatic expressions and icy poses of marble statuary, the necrotic, grave-damp churches. She and John spend winter afternoons excavating scarlet and blue plaster bits from thistle and mud, evenings at the Sargents', polishing bits of stained marble and worn coins, some pried up from rubbish heaps, bright green and smooth as cabbage leaves, others a sober brown, roughened by verdigris and grime. Violet cleans her coins with oil, varnish, and gum, rubbing at them with pieces of silk wool or bits of kid glove, uncovering, if she is lucky, the profile of Nero or Marcus Aurelius, while listening to Mrs. Sargent, that Spirit of Localities, read aloud the myth of the serpent king, or some other fantastical tale, seated deep within an armchair upholstered in exotic fabric—golden birds flitting among sad blue damask roses.

In the springtime come long walks with Mrs. Sargent, John, and Emily. Daylong wanderings outside Rome, walking dusty white roads overhung with bay trees, mulberry, and holm oaks, passing gated villas and vineyards, flowering almond trees, and humble *trattorie*. Their walks inside the city, less picturesque, take them past hovels whose starved inhabitants scratch with rough implements in poisonous lilac-colored soil, scenes that haunt Violet's susceptible imagination, poverty's tortured frieze wrapping itself endlessly around the cold majesty of Roman architecture, the cavernous tombs of Catholic churches—and always, she and John stopping to poke about with the tips of their umbrellas, stab at chinks between paving stones, pry up battered coins, pottery artifacts, shards of sculpture. Once, in the Villa Borghese, they came upon a desultory procession of priests in white-and-gold vestments, a straggle of alabaster-and-gilt peacocks strolling pink gravel paths, followed by Pius IX, rotund and sashed, raising a plump ringed hand, dispensing papal blessings among the low garden hedges and inky cypress trees, his benediction lost in the plashing of marble fountains with velvety mossed sides. Violet has given herself over to Rome's extremes, to the city's poverties and pageantries, and stops on one of her walks to watch as thousands of starlings pulse out a black disintegrating language against the white nacreous sky.

At the Sargents', John and Violet take turns reading aloud from Becker's *Gallus*, Ampère's *Histoire Romaine à Rome*, John Murray's *Handbook for Travelers*, Sir William Smith's *A Smaller Dictionary of Greek and Roman Antiquities*. In Dr. Sargent's high-ceilinged bedroom, they sing impromptu melodies of Rossini or Verdi—Violet's nasal warbling interrupted by the call to dessert, charlotte russe this time, minarets of whipped cream on golden sponge biscuit, awaiting them in the candlelit dining room. Violet's reading has become prodigious; she adores Hawthorne's *Marble Faun*, William Wetmore Story's *Roba di Roma*. Inspired mainly by these two, she writes and publishes her first story, "Les Aventures d'une pièce de monnaie," by Mlle. V.P.—a clever tale of the life of one coin, a single denarius from the reign of Hadrian. At fourteen, Violet has begun to fulfill the oath she had sworn over the sparrow, cold on its bed of pomegranate seed in the Villa Borghese: To be a writer.

V.

If you are first pronounced an ugly child, then a repulsive-looking young woman, you learn to put forth compensating virtues; in my case, a marvelous brain. My intelligence was formidable; I used it as shield and sword. In other words, if I was not to be pretty, then neither would I be "nice." I could not afford to be, and by seventeen was publishing works of precocious maturity. My half brother, Eugene, in letters first from Oxford, later from his diplomatic post in Paris, took to addressing me as "the Precocity," when he wasn't using the family's pet name, "Baby," or, worse, the odious "Bags."

Apart from my brain, I was timid. With it, I learned to strike awe, if not cerebral terror, into people twice my age. I dismissed rote courtesies, female manners, all those insidious social arts that exist in any age, principally to defang one. I displayed erudition like a peacock's iridescent-eyed tail, fanning and preening. A strutting monologist, I delighted, bored and insulted many people for many years. I apologized when necessary, never learned abjection, received no absolution. Shrank back from what I saw on people's faces— revulsion, curiosity, pity—when they beheld a female face as unlovely (some said malformed) as mine. Feigned indif-ference, although Beauty—in art, music, philosophy, litera-ture, in living women—came to obsess me. Her unfortunate antithesis, I wrote expertly of Beauty and sought out female beauty, female affection, a habit begun with Franziska, my childhood nurse, later with my governess, Marie. With the poet Mary Robinson, my worship was half-reciprocated. Only with Mary, and later with Kit, did I dare take off my brain, like a hat. Talk was camouflage, intended to enthrall persons well beyond my age and minor achievements.

As for lovely Sylvia, I grasp the irony of my present condi-tion. I cannot use grand gestures. I cannot be erudite. I cannot even be heard. Doubtless it is a mercy I am invisible. All my charm must be confined to subtlety, my seduction to influence, the genius loci, to the great female soul that is Palmerino.

Sylvia

---⊗⊗⊗---

W HEN SHE THINKS OF PHILIP, it is less with anger than with a kind of low wonder at the turn her life has taken. The past three days, seeing words, pages of words, accumulate first beneath her pen, then transferred to her laptop, has been solid comfort. Work as solace. She'd forgotten.

This morning, standing at her window, she sees Remo, in baggy shorts and sandals, trundling a wheelbarrow out from between two rows of the vegetable garden, a gray cat close at his heels. The day is sunny, promising, so she decides to forgo work and walk to the local *pasticceria* for coffee.

After washing her face and neck with an old cracked bar of lemon soap, loosely pinning up her hair ("Judas hair," Philip had called it, the shade of red associated with Christ's betrayer and less commonly with Mary Magdalene), she dresses, gathers her purse, pens, notebook, goes out. The graveled driveway, patched with invasive grass and clover, scarcely wide enough for a small Italian car, is hedged on either side with stunted pink rosebushes, rosemary, mint, lavender. Rising behind these somewhat ratty shrubs are the large trees, locust, oak, and elm, with volunteer fruit trees, apple, pear, plum, fig, mixed in . . . everything barely cared for, the kind of garden Vernon Lee preferred, secretive, struggling, with secluded groves and bowered, entangled shelters. In her last years, isolated by deafness, poor health, and the deaths of most of her friends, Vernon wandered the gardens she'd once designed, sat on the stone benches. Had, in her final days, let everything go.

At the bottom of the winding driveway, Sylvia uses Giustina's key to unlock the iron gates. The road, via il Palmerino, is exactly as she remembers it from the summer before, when she and Philip had walked the half mile or so to catch a city bus into Florence. Half an hour's walk alongside the creek, Lungo l'Affrico, before crossing the street to the popular working-class café, where men stand elbow-to-elbow along the marble counter or crowded around small round tables, drinking espressos, reading newspapers. The purchase of bus tickets, the twenty-minute ride to Piazza San Marco, the short walk to the Duomo. Funny, how precisely she recalls it all.

Via il Palmerino, heavily shaded in places, is so twisting and narrow that infrequently passing cars give warning honks before each curve to alert drivers, bicyclists, the few pedestrians like Sylvia. Mostly, she has the road to herself this morning, the walk peaceful, quiet but for birdsong. Villas along the way are concealed behind high gates and stone walls, rows of spearlike black cypress mixed in with the broad, spreading umbrella cypress. Scattered among the surrounding hills are palatial villas, deceptively small, simple-looking blocks of pale gold, bisque, or fawn. Even before coming upon the broad turn in the road where via il

Palmerino becomes Lungo l'Affrico, Sylvia hears water flowing, the abrupt drop to the creek protected by a low stone wall. On the opposite side of the stream are sprawling shrubs of wild berries, a high, leafy scrim of trees. If she's fortunate, a mallard or crested heron might break from that greenness or skim up, shattering the water's surface. On their walks, she and Philip had seen both. Long portions of the low wall are cloaked with dark star-shaped ivy, others blanketed in plush moss, black-speckled islands of bronze, green, or citrine. Lizards with white-and-black mosaic skins striped with emerald bask, jeweled brooches, on sunny ledges of the wall, vanish in swift flashes between rock crevices or down the creek side of the wall when she passes by. Small, plain butterflies, some black, most white, flit in and out of flowering weeds, linger longest before the pink soft-pursed mouths of woodbine, the moist, blooded throats of trumpet vine.

At the end of the quiet road, she faces a confusing intersection of traffic islands with curving roundabouts, cars zipping this way and that like toy vehicles in an amusement park. To get to the café that sells bus tickets means to dodge adroitly through traffic, to take calculated risks. She recalls Philip's anger over her hesitancy, realizes that even last summer, he must have known he would leave her. He had been short with her during most of that trip, too often clipped, irate, or chillingly polite. Perhaps it wasn't her timidity, her fear around foreign traffic that had so irritated him, but that he had to be with her at all. Well, he is with Ivan now, and she is alone, turning down a secondary road she hopes will bring her, eventually, to the *pasticceria*. Another downhill walk, passing elegant, compact villas, their louvered shutters painted chocolate brown, saffron gold, or dark green, some with discreet shrines to the Virgin set into niches along protective street walls made of umber or rose stone. Aside from having to watch for more frequent cars—drivers going to work, she supposes, or perhaps taking children to school— Sylvia indulges in the pleasurable liberty of the traveler whose one immediate task, hers at least for now, is to find the local pastry shop. Having all the time in the world, she stops to breathe in an especially lavish froth of honeysuckle spilling over a high unmortared stone wall.

Seated at a square marble-topped table with a dispiriting view of an empty street lined with nondescript shops, Sylvia decides the problem is this: Before she can describe love affairs between women, more specifically between Vernon Lee and the two women she loved, shouldn't she be able to understand such love, imagine having sex with another woman? She doubts memories of her own stifled experiences will suffice, those few girls and women she'd felt unspoken affection for, desires unexpressed. She's never had the courage to acknowledge honest instincts. For all she knows, she could be lesbian or bisexual, though the image of Philip and Ivan, naked, having sex, hovers, intrusive, around the edges of more pleasant thoughts of women. In forty-some years of adult life, she has had sex only with men, and the effort of trying to turn those few liaisons into bonds, relationships, had always proved a challenge. Her marriage to Philip, the most enduring of these, had been her most spectacular failure. Would love have been different—more lasting, satisfying—with another woman? Erotic fantasies of making love to a woman had never aroused her, yet there had been several girls, and, later on, women—ones she could easily name and still remember—for whom she had felt definite (repressed) attraction. One young woman in particular, a premed student, had surprised her on a dark stairway in their apartment building and suddenly, in the middle of a meaningless conversation, kissed her on the mouth. The shock, lovely and immediate, had been no different from her reaction to a man's kiss. Uttering some indignant remark, making a show of moral offense, she had pushed past the girl to hide her confusion. Had never spoken to her again. Who might she have been, freed of inhibition and sexual conditioning? If she had been more open to loving another woman, might her life not be better now?

And beauty. By Victorian standards, Violet Paget had been judged an exceptionally ugly child. Sylvia had read one account (disclaimed by several scholars) of Violet, as a little girl of seven or eight, concealed behind a curtain in her parents' drawing room, overhearing visiting friends of her mother's remark, thinking they were alone, "What a strange, ill-favored little girl . . . Poor Matilda, how will she manage with such an ugly child?" These opinions did not abate as Violet grew older. They grew worse. She suffered cruel asides and pitying looks, most often from men. Women, on the whole, were more sympathetic. If her social awkwardness and physical timidity were aspects of a crippling self-consciousness, then her first infatuation, with Mary Robinson, could have remained chaste. In recent writings about Vernon Lee, several scholars presumed a fully sexual life for her. Sylvia wasn't convinced.

In nineteenth-century England, young unmarried women, "properly raised," required female companions to accompany them outside of their homes. Many of these companions became intimate friends, their affections expressed in ornate, cloying, even suggestive terms. Did such friendships sometimes include sex? The standard Victorian view was that women, by their natures, were nonphysical beings. If Vernon was ever sexual, it would far likelier have been with the high-spirited Kit Anstruther-Thomson, not with Mary, whose fey, poetic temperament fell within the bounds of Victorian convention. Besides, Sylvia had learned from her own painful marriage that denial is its own complicity, and nearly anything could be true of anybody.

She pays for her coffee and leaves, making her way to Essa Lunga, a nearby supermarket. Walking along the broad tree-lined avenue of this modern suburb outside Florence (she doesn't even know its name), passing undistinguished shops and plain apartment buildings, she entertains a brief thought of moving to Italy, of living here. When Philip offered to buy her out of her half of their home, she had initially hesitated. But once she realized how often he had secretly entertained Ivan in their home, in her bed, on occasions when she was out of town doing research, giving a reading somewhere, or, worse, tending to each of her dying parents, she couldn't move out fast enough. She had put her things—surprisingly few beyond books and a few pieces of her parents' furniture—in storage and come here.

The supermarket is all tight aisles jammed with people steering wire carts, grimly bumping and shoving their way along. She feels disembodied even as she places a bottle of

Chianti, a box of fettuccine, a jar of tomato sauce, some yogurt, apples, salad, a baguette, laundry detergent, and some dark Swiss chocolate in her own cart. Unable to communicate beyond the most childish request or basic sentence, she feels a flare of panic as she angles among shoppers, no one particularly friendly toward, or tolerant of, her presence. And not for the first time, Sylvia chides herself for not having made a more serious attempt to learn Italian.

Her panic eases after she emerges onto the street with her plastic bags. Practically trudging uphill, she feels like the cliché of an elderly Italian widow, dressed, no matter the season, in black, carrying net bags of groceries, grim, stubborn, determined to survive. The image makes her shudder. Switching bags from hand to hand, repositioning the shoulder strap of her purse, favoring the newly blistered heel of her right foot, she makes her way to the villa.

By the time she unlocks the iron gates, the sky is freighted with black clouds, and thunder rolls, ominous, in the distance. When the rain comes, accompanied by rough, tearing winds and a wild shattering of hail that will ruin at least a third of the grapes in Remo's vineyard, Sylvia will be upstairs, watching from her open window, drinking the local wine, eating the baguette she bought, cocooned in one of Giustina's shapeless black sweaters.

After the storm dies down to a steadier rain, with the air in her room feeling cool and vibrantly green, she sits down to describe, as best she can, Violet's first love, first vulnerability, Mary Robinson.

Mary Robinson

Casa Paget
12 via Solferino
Florence
September 1873

As a young British diplomat in Lisbon, Eugene Lee-Hamilton's ennui manifests in increasingly painful sensitivities to light and sound, chest spasms, and a string of calf-sick letters to Matilda. . . . "Dearest little Mamma," he writes, "my little ducky darling, how happy we shall be when I am finally with thee!"

Addressing her son as "Beloved of My Heart, Life of My Soul," Matilda urges Eugene to eat meat, keep to himself, think only of her. "At the thought of thy being ill, I myself am in an ague. Hast thou quinine pills with thee? If not, pray immediately desire a druggist to make thee up a scruple in twenty pills. Hast thou a good soup for luncheon daily? Didst thou get the saucepan? For God's sake, let thy bones, muscles, brain, and spirits have all the help that Beef (and Sleep sufficient) can afford. How I miss thee!"

So when offered the insult of a backwater post in Bue-
nos Aires, Eugene takes the opportunity to resign and be
transported home to his mother on a litter, accompanied
by a male attendant, his legs and back suddenly, bafflingly,
paralyzed.

In the meantime, after years of restless migration, the
Paget family has perched itself in a cavernous, gloomy Florentine apartment near the Mugnone canal, the leafy trees
of the Cascine beckoning like a sibilant chorus of green-
haired naiads at the end of an otherwise stony street. When
he arrives home at 12 via Solferino, twenty-eight-year-old
Eugene is finished. The world no longer suits him, and he
has ceased all movement in it. Instead, he lies faceup on a
rolling bier, a metal and wood gurney. At first, he can only
be spoken to, whispered to, in no more than five words at a
time. His faux corpse demands scheduled spoon feedings,
being read aloud to, much petting and tendering of famil-
ial kisses. While his stepfather, Mr. Paget, departs (escapes)
every morning at half past eight to sit for hours in the café
at the Santa Maria di Novella train station, reading foreign
newspapers and observing the comings and goings of travelers, Mrs. Paget and sixteen-year-old Violet remain home
to respond dutifully to Eugene's ceaseless torrent of needs.

As horizontal despot and vatic demigod, Eugene takes
it upon himself to oversee Violet's education. He devises
daily schoolroom exercises for her: an essay on the political
decline of the Dutch republic, for example, or a commentary on his own unpublished article on Pope Sixtus V, urban
planner and designer of the Vatican Library.

Violet ventures out-of-doors in the company of a female servant only during the late afternoons, after she has finished reading aloud to Eugene, copied down his dictated poems and letters, heard his lofty critique on her latest attempt at scholarship. His paralysis is tyranny, a chronic inclemency inside the house. His rule goes unquestioned, since pity is at its root, along with Violet's unappeasable guilt for being healthy, whole-limbed, and secretly furious with everyone in her family.

Casa Paget
12 via Solferino
Florence
October 1880

With a faint rustle of her maroon-and-black-striped faille skirt, Mary Robinson trails her parents up a cool staircase leading to the Pagets' lodgings on via Solferino. Glad to escape the unseasonal heat of an October afternoon, she is eager to make the acquaintance of the Pagets, rumored to be an intellectually rigorous, if peculiar, family. At the insistence of a friend who had recommended them, Mr. and Mrs. Robinson have accepted an invitation to tea at the Paget residence before returning to London. They have just come from Venice, where Mary was introduced to Henry Layard, an archaeologist whose discoveries at Nineveh had so fascinated her at the British Museum, as well as to Ernest Renan, the heretical French philosopher, theologian, and Orientalist. Mary has just published her first volume of poetry, *A Handful of Honeysuckle*, and with her innate confidence further bolstered by adoring parents, she has assumed a tenuous place on the lower rung of London's literary circles.

In response to Mr. Robinson's firm knock, a female servant draws open the massive black door to the Paget residence. Mary follows her parents into an imposing north-lit room with ornate embossed ceilings, a series of high, narrow windows swagged with crimson satin brocade, and a purplish marble mosaic floor. Yellow roses bloom from various antique painted pots, and a quantity of dark, carved eighteenth-century furniture is placed, with no apparent plan, about the room—including a priest's confessional box, uncurtained and piled with firewood. In the midst of this shadowy, storybook atmosphere sits a slight young woman with golden brown wavy hair, her inquisitive gray eyes strangely magnified by a fantastic pair of huge eighteenth-century green goggles. Violet Paget stands, stretches out a hand, the slim white fingers emerging like petals from the cutting immobility of her black dress's severe cuff, and greets each of her guests by turn. (For her part, Violet is struck by the young creature rippling toward her, holding a dainty lace-edged parasol. The otherworldly luminosity, the charismatic dark eyes limpid with sympathy—exactly how she has always pictured the baron's clever daughter in Scheffel's *Der Trompeter von Säkkingen*!)

The first hour passes in glittering arpeggios of polite conversation accompanied by cups of black tea and milk, followed in the second hour by biscotti and glasses of *vin santo*. From his horizontal pulpit, Eugene tells in a delicate, oratorical whisper, more breath than sound, the latest tattle on his little sister, Violet. Just yesterday, he whispers, she had crouched in the garden shrubbery beneath an open window while their mother, sitting at her piano near that same window, tinkled out the crystalline opening notes of an eighteenth-century song, "Pallido il sole," Hasse's piece, famously sung by the castrato Farinelli to mad King Philip of Spain—music that had arrived by post that morning. Unwrapping the paper parcel from Bologna, Violet declared that her reputation hung on this one composition, and had handed the score to her mother before hurtling downstairs into the garden to hear each note as it floated through the window, released from ivory and black keys by the imperious, agile pressure of Matilda's fingers. Moments later, Violet crept upstairs to further listen through the cool plaster wall of an adjoining room, against which first her left, then her right ear pressed flat. Hasse's song proved superb, thus preserving the theories she had set forth in *Studies of the Eighteenth Century in Italy*, published earlier that year by W. Satchell and Co., London.

Mary Robinson listens to Eugene whisper on about his sister, thinking what a paradox she is, this small, strange-looking Violet Paget. All outward timidity and childlike vulnerability, yet bristling, picketed, by a ferocious, encyclopedic, old mind.

The next day, Mr. and Mrs. Robinson acquiesce to Mary's and Violet's pleading and leave for London without their daughter. They have agreed to let Mary stay on with the Paget family, though, as they later discuss between themselves on the train, the household is nothing if not bizarre, what with the brother broadcasting from his rolling bed like some hermaphroditic Roman pedant, only the large, slipshod mouth moving, and the tiny mother, embalmed in the resin of eighteenth-century fashion and speech, straight down to her oyster-colored bobbing ringlets and strange Quaker usage of *thee* and *thou*!—followed by the Byronesque father (what was his name?), mute as stone but for an occasional non sequitur regarding the superior hunting and fishing to be had in a place called Thun, and finally, young Violet, her opinions and recitations erupting lavalike from a brain of seeming universal capacity and in such a stammering, pinched, unfortunate voice that her physical composition, poor child—that great jutting jaw, porcine eyes, and thin suet-colored hair—is only further accentuated. Still, they saw no harm in Mary's forming an otherwise brilliant acquaintance.

The Robinsons' afternoon visit had been a mere foretaste of their daughter's monthlong stay with the Pagets, a sojourn Mary will detail in a barrage of daily letters to her parents. Imagine, she writes, a household existing only to debate opinions of art, music, poetry, and philosophy, a family (aside from the father, who is largely absent) breathing only, morning till night, for the disciplined pleasures of the intellect. Mary describes late-morning excursions in a landau specially kitted out for Eugene, a smoothed plank laid across the sides so that he can lie prone upon it, how she and Violet perch on either side, vestal creatures, shading Eugene's broad, pallid face with black silk parasols while Beppe, with his team of bays, drives them out of Florence, high into the pastoral hills and winding streams of San Gervasio along a dirt road following Lungo l'Affrico, the very stream referenced in Boccaccio's *Decameron*! Sometimes she and Violet climb down from the cart to gather arm-loads of forget-me-nots, reeds, boughs of spindle wood, small bunches of grape hyacinth and wreathe Eugene's straw hat with loose garlands of wildflowers. In one let-ter, Mary attempts to convey the atmosphere of the Paget salons, the parade of stellar visitors—the Italians (Carlo Placci, Enrico Nencioni), the Russians (Peter Boutour-line), the French (Anatole France!), the Americans and the British (Henry James, Aldous Huxley), the Germans (Karl Hillebrand, Adolf von Hildebrand)—really, she can't be expected to remember them all—glittering constellations of sculptors, critics, composers, poets, translators, musicians, diplomats, novelists, and always, there comes that last, ines-capable salon hour when Matilda Paget, a demiregal doll creature, faded ringlets bouncing, attacks her piano's key-board, everyone in the room made to listen to the explosive or subsiding end, of Beethoven, Schubert, or Scarlatti. In one letter to her parents, Mary quotes Eugene, how he had opined during that day's luncheon, with a sour expulsion of air from his lungs, that "invalidism, like infection, breeds sublime poetry." The horizon, he labored on, was his sin-gular vantage point. Fastened to his board by day, wheeled about by servants, sideways and aslant, at night, in dreams, he is upright, walking freely. . . . "I speak from the perspec-tive of the dead, though I am as yet unburied. There are twelve types of horizon I have discovered and given name to. . . ." This, Mary writes, is one manner in which Eugene might open a conversation with whoever is near—in this case, herself. His poetry, what she has read of it, is sluggish, black-veined stuff, tragic as drowning. The poems, she confides to her parents, seem overinfluenced by Poe and Baudelaire; several are morbidly tinctured with self-pity.

She writes nothing of Eugene's sister, because she has fallen in love with her. And because in Violet, who has begun to use the pseudonym Vernon Lee ("Let us admit that any male writer shall always receive more attention than a female"), Mary has discovered a friend whose knowledge of music, literature, and art surpasses her own. Has ever such a gorgeous mind issued forth from a mere woman, Mary marvels, writing in her private journal by the thin, sallow light of a bedside candle. Being with Violet is intoxicating, how Mary imagines it must have been to be in the presence of the French Symbolist poet Verlaine. Vernon—she really must stop calling her Violet—expounds easily on any manner of subjects in any of four subtly conjugated languages, French, German, English, and the Tuscan dialect of Dante. The breadth and depth of her friend's intelligence, enfolded, engraved deep within her young brain, can never be fully sounded; it settles around Mary like a cloak or climate, like some infinite and liberating perspective. And though Mary sometimes hears her friend's verbal wit descend into cruel impatience, she still admires her. If Vernon cannot abide hypocrisy, must attack and undo it with pitiless words, is there not rough honor in that? Aware her own ideas and opinions are diluted with counterfeit kindness, Mary is inspired, watching Vernon brandish her way through dense thickets of social nicety and dead form.

Their month together passes quickly, and on the morning she must leave, Mary extracts a promise from Vernon that she will visit London the following spring and stay with Mary in her parents' home on Gower Street, a mere twenty-minute walk from the marvels and antiquities of the British Museum.

The Robinson House
84 Gower Street
London
June 1881

Downstairs in the stifling hot, cabbage-stinking kitchen, two of Mr. Robinson's servants trade vulgar jokes about the unmannered, queerly dressed young woman who appeared on the doorstep in the middle of lunch, surrounded by an impossible number of trunks and boxes, and now has everyone dashing upstairs and down to suit her peremptory, unpredictable demands. Several of her boxes still sit in the already-cramped foyer, even as the first guests arrive for yet another of the Robinsons' *tertulias,* or salons. Lonely, widowed Mr. Browning, a wispy nimbus of white hair swirling about his head, followed by aesthete Mr. Wilde with his ink-stained yellow kid gloves and silk knee breeches, the Rossettis, William and Lucy, Leslie Stephens—or any of the others, equally famous or bent upon such fame. They step down from carriages, gather on the steps, knock upon the Robinsons' scarlet door, London's finest writers, artists, musicians, critics. And sometime within the next hour, the Robinsons' noxious new houseguest will descend the staircase and forge her way, with flagrant ambition, all around the drawing room, her erudition needling forth in a nasal

whine, turning old heads, pricking up old ears, what relent-
less intelligence!—astonishing, off-putting. A shock. At the
moment, however, this creature with a man's name is still
upstairs, demanding a servant shoehorn her petulant feet
into a new, untried pair of boy's black boots.

In her tight new boots, Vernon paces the bedroom overlooking Gower Street, waiting for Mary to escort her
downstairs, introduce her to the elite of London's literary
world. Some of that world, anyway. She yanks the black
tasseled cord, belling for a second cup of chamomile tea,
sits to scrawl a hasty, up-slanting note of assurance to her
mother and invalid brother (presently taking the water cure
in Bagni di Lucca) that she is quite well and will describe
more of her London debut the following day. Her digestion
is in turmoil. Drawing down the cord a second, brisk time,
she repeats her demand for tea. Strains of Mozart's Diver-
timento in D Major, wafting upstairs from the hired string
quartet, are obliterated by a clattering of carriage wheels,
the iron-shod hooves of horses on cobblestones outside the
Robinson home, followed by guttural shouts of cabbies and
low, murmurous exchanges between guests being helped
down from their cabs.

"Viol— Vernon! You look wickedly, wickedly smart!"
Mary comes into the room, bringing the tea herself, since
the servants have refused to lift one more finger for that
exasperating person upstairs.

"Everyone is mad to meet you. Apparently, it is de
rigueur in London to be *seen* with a copy of your brilliant
Studies of the Eighteenth Century in Italy. No one can believe

the author of such an important book is half most of their ages—you have quite put the old knobs to shame!"

Pleased, Vernon takes the tea from Mary. Just as she'd dreamed, London's aging literary lions, purring at her feet!

She sips at the pale gold tea, spilling some across the bodice of her black silk dress as she stands before the looking glass, attempting, with one hand, to loosen the white Gladstone collar—her outfit deliberately devised to look mannish but not manly. This, she explains to Mary, is how a mind—her mind—looks when it is personified, dressed. By contrast, Mary is the ideal late-Victorian beauty in a peony pink lawn dress with a high bustle, her mass of chestnut curls freshly coiffed, her alabaster skin and large, sympathetic brown eyes. Standing on tiptoe at the mullioned window, looking down to the street, she merrily relays back to Vernon the various names and titles of the guests arriving now in rapid succession—Mr. and Mrs. William Morris . . . taciturn, waspy old Thomas Hardy, the Rossettis . . . —interspersing tidbits of gossip with exclamations over the darkening skies, a summer storm that will surely drench the ladies' dresses, soak through and ruin their satin slippers.

As the youngest daughter of George Robinson, a wealthy banker popular for what he calls his *tertulias,* after the Spanish *tertulia,* or evening party, Mary, at twenty-four, is already a minor poetess. Her father's parties bring all of London's au courant writers and artists under one roof, and Mary is known for her ability to charm and soften the dourest, most intractable of her father's famous guests. Vernon will mainly prove adept at succinct, callous assessments of others, her sociability of a more detrimental nature than her friend's. A prodigy at twenty-five, she has already published a number of distinctive essays, and her single book, *Studies of the Eighteenth Century in Italy*, is the talk of literary London, its author regarded as a mystery of precocious female intelligence. This afternoon, those who wish to meet this enigmatic creature have gathered in George Robinson's drawing room, where Mary is only too eager to show off her new, unusual friend.

But the Gower Street *tertulia* proves a disappointing manifestation of Mary's glowing predictions. No one is at Vernon's feet, although, as she later consoles herself, neither is she at any of theirs. True, she is greeted respectfully, with mild deference, but the power of masculine achievement hangs like granite in the room, and the young female author of a single book finds she must scrap as hard or harder than anyone for a share of attention. Physically slight, severe but loquacious, Vernon attracts mixed attention in her black dress with its high, stiff white collar, her bird-cropped hair, her spectacles adding an intimidating glint to already-piercing eyes. As promised, she writes to Matilda and Eugene the next morning, inflating the impression she has made, belittling several of the "august" persons she was introduced to. In the weeks to come, as a guest of the Robinsons, she will further recount, in lashing scrawls of brown ink, details and gossip concerning receptions, teas, dinner parties, trips to the theater, excursions to Oxford and the nearby British Museum, scroll through an impressive roster of the publishers, editors, writers, and artists she has met, largely due to the generosity of her hosts. No matter how privately she dislikes some of these people, they are "persons to cultivate," contacts necessary to her literary reputation. Dispensing scurrilous gossip and arch description in equal measure, she entertains her invalid brother and insatiable mother, both ravenous for news of London's celebrities. After an evening with Mary at the Royal Academy's opening of a Pre-Raphaelite exhibition, Vernon recounts the absurdity of clothing and mannerism—never has she seen, she writes, so many plain women stepping so grandly or pretentiously out of carriages ... "crazy-looking creatures: one with crinkled gauze all tied close about her & with visibly no underclothes (& a gold laurel wreath!), another with ivy leaves tied to each other's stalks to create a garland on her short, horrid, red hair; another with a trimming and necklace of marigolds & parsley fern on thread, a lot of insane slashing and stomachings ... and one fair-haired sylph, draped entirely in fishing net, seashells and moss, nothing more!"

She describes, more tenderly, a visit she and Mary paid to Robert Browning at his sister's home in Maida Vale. It was pouring rain out, so they stayed some hours with Mr. Browning, who showed them his late wife Elizabeth's Greek lesson book, so tiny that it fit neatly inside Vernon's hand. She and Mr. Browning find they share a love of Italy, a common friend in Enrico Nencioni, translator of Robert's and Elizabeth's poetry. Poor, lonely Mr. Browning, she wrote, keeps up a murmuring, tireless stream of talk. One dares not interrupt him for fear he might cease to breathe. Talk, and talk alone, keeps him knit together.

In one unusually cheerful missive, Violet describes introducing Mary to her friend John Sargent, of the portrait he virtually dashes off in one afternoon, a "quite fierce and cantankerous looking Vernon Lee," a likeness she very much approves of. They are invited to tea in his art studio, along with Mr. Walter Pater, dear mole, "limping from gout," with his two sisters, Hester and Clara, each wearing "fantastic apple-green dresses," and Mr. Henry James, who keeps "wrinkling his forehead over his too-tight boots."

While courting recognition from those people in London who "matter," Violet's true fascination lies with Mary, whose admirers grumble that even as Miss Robinson shines beautifully, by contrast, beside that crude sketch of Vernon Lee, she grows more remote, less accessible, due to that creature's horrid fawning. All summer, Mary is adored, sought after, while Vernon, publically commended for her massive brain, is privately loathed, even mocked, for her egregious manner. Mannish. Bellicose. A gargoyle. People, mainly men, are unkind. Even the Robinsons have grown weary of their strange guest, of the turmoil she throws their house into. Following a particularly sharp quarrel with Mr. Robinson over what Vernon insists is a trifling matter, Vernon commands the Robinsons' servants to pack up her things, and, with Mary in docile tow, decamps to Sussex, where she has secured a small thatched cottage, utterly quiet, far from anyone.

The Robinson House
84 Gower Street
London
July 1881

Mr. Robinson assumes his deepest, most draconian voice. "I will countenance this no longer!" Vernon, wearing Mary's borrowed red satin bed wrapper, hangs over the carved banister, shamelessly eavesdropping.

"... impertinent. She 'forgot,' so she says, to ask her cousin to write a letter of permission. More importantly, she asked no permission of me, none at all, simply assuming she could annex our Mary and spirit her off to Paris. I accept the girl is arrogant by nature, that she cannot help herself, that she is Mary's closest friend, but this goes too far."

Soothing, futile imprecations from Mrs. Robinson, followed by silence.

Then:

"No. This house is too small with her in it. Our family harmony has been compromised. We've welcomed her too long, and she has taken advantage. You will find a way to tell her."

Voices, one angry, one pleading, recede; a door crashes shut.

Vernon creeps back to her room, not hers anymore, apparently. Bosh. Tempests in teapots. And why? Because I neglected to ask my cousin, Lydia, to write to Mr. Robinson asking permission for Mary to travel with me to Lydia's home in Paris? And the day before, that asinine quarrel with Mary's sister, Monica, over a perceived snub at not being invited along to an artist's reception, though she had earlier insisted she was loath to go. Vernon thought to spare Monica by not inviting her. Monica had wept noisily to her mother, who took offense; then the whole household erupted. Such things never happened in the Paget household, no broodings, mopings, explosions of ill temper; everyone did as they pleased, trodding on one another's toes so thoughtlessly that calluses, not bruises, were the norm. Better for everyone. The Robinson household is a thin-shelled goose egg, shattering at the least tap to its deceptively smooth surface. Vernon newly appreciates her own household, her father's daily disappearance into the woods with his hunting gun and fishing rod or to the train station rather than pretend to hold sway over his gabbling wife and voluble, high-opinioned children. Suddenly, Vernon misses the impartial, invigorating waters of the Paget home. She pulls on the bell cord for someone to help dress her, wonders if Mary has yet heard about her father's decree. Does she know that Mr. Robinson has gone to work and left his wife the chore of suggesting to Vernon that she seek other lodgings?

Well, this unwanted guest will leave before being officially—and officiously—told that she must. She is nothing if not resourceful, and between her and Mary, they have a host of mutual friends to call on for assistance.

A plan assembles itself so quickly that by the time Mr. Robinson arrives home for his Thursday luncheon of cold pickled beef tongue and red beet salad, he is met with news that Mary and Vernon have hired a cottage near Pulborough in Sussex for a fortnight and will be gone by morning.

As he is handed this bittersweet digestive by his wife, Vernon is already upstairs packing—or rather, having three servants pack for her, as she is busy, composing two letters, one to her mother and brother, another to Mr. Robinson, a profuse (to mask its insincerity) apology for her aberrant manners, peccadilloes, et cetera. Piff and toff, she thinks. All for dear Mary's sake, keeping the peace.

In truth, she is elated by the prospect of she and Mary, alone with their books, notebooks, clothing, taking up uninterrupted residence together in the countryside. Two quarrels, yesterday's and today's, have produced this one boon. Fourteen days and nights in the English countryside, alone with Mary, free of the Robinsonian glare. Mary, too, is packing, downstairs in the kitchen, ensuring provisions for tomorrow's journey, sandwiches of the same pickled tongue with mustard, fresh tomatoes, a leek and veal pie, sweet plum cake, and six brown glass bottles of lemonade.

Sussex
England
July 1881

Upon unlocking the door and stepping inside the shadowy main room, they find the cottage hideously quaint, mildewed, and plagued by mice. Yet it is theirs, bowered by wild eglantine and clematis; it is theirs with a bit of cleaning, fuel for lamps, and a stone jar of fresh-picked wildflowers. And Mary, Vernon writes to Matilda, is a positive siren of domesticity. They are so much happier here than on Gower Street; already, three days have shot by in pastoral bliss. They write, read, walk, have picnics beneath great sheltering trees, and, on rare occasion, speak to a neighbor passing by the cottage. They wake and sleep as they please; Vernon wears trousers with a broadcloth workshirt and has already had Mary crop her hair twice as short as it was. Mary goes without stays or corset—cutting, Vernon writes, a perfect Kate Greenaway figure.

On their second night, Vernon lies awake, thinking of Mary, whose bedroom is across the hall, only a few steps away.

"Mary?"

Within the carved four-poster bed, the bedcoverings shift as Mary half sits, propped on her elbows, hair dropping back from one shoulder in a single thick braid. Vernon suddenly remembers her childhood nurse, Franziska, how her creamy blond braids smelled of cinnamon pastry. Wonders what became of her.

"There is the most hideous brown insect flitting about my room. I'm afraid it may get into the bed. May I climb in with you for a bit?"

Half-asleep, Mary makes a space for her friend to climb in beside her. The bed is not large.

Listening to her friend's slow, even breathing, unable to see Mary's waist-length braided hair or her great dark eyes, closed in sleep, eyes that by day take in the world without censure, sweeten observation into poetry without any sacrifice of intelligence. Kindness may be Mary's weakness, Vernon thinks, but she wishes she could learn to see the world in half so soft a light.

The next afternoon, carrying a wicker hamper between them to a spot beside the nearby creek, they spread an oilcloth-backed merino blanket beneath a grove of mature oaks, unpack brown bread, white cheddar cheese, strawberries, cherries, and bottles of ginger beer. After lunch, Mary stands and, steadying herself against a tree trunk, unlaces both shoes, rolls down and strips off her stockings, unbuttons and steps out of her green striped dress. Wearing only a muslin chemise and pantalettes, she picks her way, barefoot, down to the creek, wades in without hesitating, straight up to her waist. Turns to Vernon, her slim white arms flung wide, and says with a laugh . . . "If only I could swim, I'd be a silver minnow for the day!"

That night, Vernon lies a second time beside Mary in bed, having again used the fabrication, the lie, about insects. She recalls the timbre of Mary's laughter, her arms bare, glazed with creek water, her face flushed from the afternoon sun. Vernon's heart bears her along, as if toward a precipice, toward feelings she fears she cannot control, toward longings that threaten to tear her to pieces. Were there no books to master this sort of storm, no studies, no lessons to learn ways to subdue and restrain desire? Or must she simply endure lying beside Mary, heart thudding fast, hardly breathing, the narrow span between their bodies an impassable gulf?

She knows Mary's affections for her are chaste, uncorrupted by the fevered, unnatural impulses that course, alien, through her own body, exhausting her. One night, as if sensing her friend's torment, Mary nests her smaller hand in Vernon's, exerts upon her friend's fingers a sweet pressure, which Vernon, trembling, silent, returns.

Love exerts its magnetism. Beauty is private, iridescent. Their gaiety is coy, has a sly, hysteric edge, and they profess adoration for each other twenty times a day. Every night, they lie close in thick cottage darkness, naked beneath sheer cambric layers of nightclothes, sensation curbed, contained in the delicate matching of fingertips, the subtlest of pressures given and returned.

V.

⸺⸻⸺

Io mi domando. I ask myself. What is the shortest tributary into empathy—imagination or experience?

Is not empathy that consciousness leading us, unwitting, into the realm of spirits, avatars, even demons?

Are not the dead still trying to reach the living?

I watch her write with tortured hesitation, doubting her construct of fact and fiction. Yet even as she doubts, she still arrives at the boundary of what I call the <u>Akashic</u>, the dimension where I now live. Imagination leads more swiftly to empathy than experience, and empathy brings Sylvia nearer to me. It is a kind of mediumship, empathy, and like any medium or "sensitive," Sylvia's accuracy can be flawed by projection, distraction, simple fatigue. Still, isn't this what writers do superlatively and all of the time: slip free of self, enter another?

Allow me to explain:

When I lie beside Mary's tight-budded beauty, my fingertips against hers, she breathes with happy, untroubled conscience while I imagine the shape and taste of her lips, her breasts, her dark source. My longing to break into her innocence horrifies me. I can scarcely fight off images, imagined scenes of passion that grow wilder with each passing hour, as if a devil were instructing me in all that I might do with her. How I might ruin her. She sleeps; I rage. Yet each day, I throw myself anew into a pretense, distort myself into Mary Robinson's perfect companion. Whenever her back is turned, though, I gaze at her with what feels like vile, hollow-eyed craving. When she turns to speak to me, I am all smooth charm, courtesy.

It was at the Sussex cottage I got up the courage to dress like a man. Just as I had given myself a man's name— Vernon Lee—I reasoned that if I could not possess Mary bodily, due to the sameness of our sex (and the offense of my desire) I could fancy myself a man beside her, seething on the inside, debonair on the surface. Of Mary's many admirers, I was the finest. Why? Because I could mix the sweet intimacies of female friendship with the excitable friction, the liberties, of a man.

You try too hard, Sylvia, to imagine yourself a "repressed Victorian lesbian," to quote the most recent, asinine scholar. While I admire your industry, I pity your failure. I have decided to help.

A silver cat, large and old, pads into your room, leaps onto your writing desk; as you stroke her head, her eyes, green, hard, gleaming, stare into yours.

Sylvia

B<small>ECAUSE SHE COMES DOWNSTAIRS</small> at the same time each morning, Remo has begun making coffee for her. This comforts Sylvia, his thoughtfulness. Today, seeing him at work in the garden, she waves. "Buongiorno, Remo! Sto andando in città." ("I am going into the city.") He straightens up, nods, and as she walks down the path toward the gate, she feels him watching her.

On the short bus ride to Florence, she feels other people watching her, too. She is dressed in a simple white linen suit, a silk scarf, heels, and has pinned her hair into a loose bun at the nape of her neck. The men and women sitting around her look weary, less in need of sleep than some miraculous occurrence—romance, fortune, exotic travel—to inject vitality back into their lives. A few stare boldly, as if estimating the value of her jewelry or her life. Only the teenagers, bounding effortlessly up the steps, shifting backpacks, cell phones to their ears, chattering, seem animated, charged with hope. The rest are husks, she thinks, consumed from the inside out.

She has two appointments, the first at the British

Institute in Palazzo Lanfredini. Breathless from climbing several steep flights of marble stairs, she is greeted by
a young woman at the front desk, ushered into a modest
room containing over four hundred books from Vernon
Lee's personal library. The archivist comes in, says she is
welcome to remove and examine any particular book from
the glass-fronted oak cabinets. Seated at a plain table, paging through each book in the stack of twenty or so volumes
she has selected, Sylvia is impressed by Vernon's massive
annotations and underlinings, remarks and responses
crammed into every margin. She'd used pencil, scribbling
in French, Italian, German, or English, depending on what
language the book was printed in. The tumultuous energy
of this woman still lives in her handwriting, swallowing
every bit of white space, her opinions ornamented with
wildly charged exclamation points, flagrant, heavy dashes.
If she presses her ear to any page, Sylvia feels she might hear
Vernon, resurrected by her own arguments, erudite, mesmerizing. When the archivist excuses herself, saying she has
to leave the room to take an overseas call, Sylvia gets up to
search quietly for a particular title she has just remembered,
slips it out from between its neighbors. Jules Romains, *Le
Couple France-Allemagne*, a slim French paperback on the
conflict over the Saar region, the book Vernon Lee was
reading on the day she died. The last book she had read.
Sylvia sits back down, and as if someone else is directing her
to do this, she drops the cream-colored book with its red-
lettered title and deckled pages into her oversized handbag.
It's hers, that's all. Vernon wants her to have it.

Back on the street, holding a piece of scrap paper with the address the receptionist had written down, she passes locked antique shops, open by appointment only, rare objects and pieces of furniture from the eighteenth and nineteenth centuries placed sparingly in display windows. Farther down via Maggio is Casa Guidi, former home of the Brownings, another place she and Philip had visited last summer. Finally, when she matches the written address with the number above a set of tall wooden doors with massive iron rings, Sylvia presses the bell, waits for the answering click, pushes open one of the doors.

The small foyer of Palazzo Corsini Suarez is dark, tenebrous. Straight ahead, a white shaft of sunlight, religious-looking, hangs suspended in a central courtyard. Going up the marble steps to her right, taking a second, then a third flight, she ascends into a cool, dim-lit rookery of marble and granite. Half of Florence, she thinks, stopping to catch her breath before climbing the fourth flight, makes a living by restoring and preserving the city's illustrious dead. What difference between a mausoleum and a Florentine building filled with the collected detritus of the vanished? It is a city of stone, of *pietra serena* and marble broken and hauled from quarries. Every street cobbled in gray or tiled in black stone. Walk any congested main street or quiet side street, ring a certain bell, hear the door click, unlock, and you step into a museum, a library, an antique shop, someone's home, vanish down a corridor and become stone yourself, heavy, implacable, cold. Stone and marble, earth's versions of eternity. Mausoleum and building, separated by breath. By breathing.

She finds the small library, its central room empty but for a woman seated before a computer at an information desk. Heavy wood and glass cabinets line all four walls, each cabinet filled with books. The ceiling is high, ornate, the library air dry and still, tinted faint amber, verdigris, honeycomb. This is one section of the Gabinetto Vieusseux, once a circulating library, reading room, and conversational gathering place for writers like George Sand, Stendahl, Schopenhauer, Dostoyevsky, Emile Zola, Mark Twain, André Gide, Thackeray, Kipling, Gertrude Stein. The Brownings, of course, who lived up the street. She can't remember them all. The main part of the Gabinetto Vieusseux is in Palazzo Strozzi, but this room, on via Maggio, houses personal book collections, papers, and letters of some of Italy's leading writers. Sylvia walks over and speaks to the woman, mentions the archivist's name from the British Institute, hoping this will bring favor. It does. The woman goes into a back room, returns with a set of pale green folders, escorts Sylvia to one of the wooden library tables. Switching on a brass desk light, she fans the dozen or so folders out in front of Sylvia. Chronologically arranged, each folder contains dozens of Vernon Lee's handwritten letters. Many are in Italian, nearly a third are addressed to her friend Countess Maria Pasolini, another group addressed to her mother, the rest to various acquaintances.

By the third folder, Sylvia's excitement sours into frustration. Penned in splotched mud brown ink, the letters are unreadable. Many are cross-written, a nineteenth-century practice used to conserve paper. Only the embossed letterhead at the top of some of the letters, *Il Palmerino, San*

Gervasio, Florence, square black lettering on cream stationery, is clear. With effort, she can parse phrases, a few short sentences. The most decipherable letter, sent from Charleton House, Scotland, in 1881, during Vernon's first visit to Kit's ancestral home, is addressed to Mrs. Paget at Casa Betti alla Villa, Bagni di Lucca. In this four-page letter, parts of sentences, sometimes whole sentences, leap forth.

> *Take care of the enclosed, it's a sweet little note, is it not, it touched me a good deal. But all the king's horses, not all the [something unreadable in Latin] can't set this right again. We are_____at sixes and sevens, Mary and I, else she wd understand that of all horrible proposals_____under that _____roof wd to me be the worse. I don't know whether she's married yet, or still on the eve of it, & trying to get patched up with me while_____still time before the thing's done. . . . Kit was very delighted with_____, she's very fond of me; and often talks of what she calls "the 'Fine China' of which you are made." Excuse the scrawl; I am writing in bed, waiting for breakfast. I am waked at half past eight, get my bath & then get into bed again as the Russian woman told me, before finishing drying. I believe I am at last going to bathe today. It came to nothing the day before yesterday, we drove round the country in the cart, but there are no bathing machines anywhere, people rushing to the sea from their houses. The sea is beautiful. I am going down today with a child to carry my towels and to prevent my clothes being_____I*

don't know whether I_____be able to bear it, as it's
a mile and a half each way. _____, I have seawa-
ter in my bath, which Hutchinson said was almost as
good_____Blackwood_____.

The letter becomes completely unreadable from there,
yet this turns out to be the most legible and lengthiest section of all the letters. She can make out salutations—"Dearest
Mamma"—and signings off—"Goodbye. E. so much Love,
V," though even Vernon's *V* is irritable, fussy-looking. She
thinks she translates something in a letter to Countess
Pasolini about taking care of her pony, then something else,
in one of the Charleton House letters to her mother:

Good luck has put me in the house of one of the most
wonderfully good and gentle and strong and simple
of all_____beings; namely this big Kit Thomson,
who talks slang like a schoolboy, cares in reality
for nothing but pictures and trees and grass and
Browning and Shelley and what is right and wrong
and why . . . you will understand why it will make
me_____miserable if I were not permitted to have
this woman in Florence. This is _____for you and
E, Somuch love, V.

Pinned to the conical light of her desk lamp, Sylvia
finds the space claustral, suffocating. Over the years and
decades, Vernon's handwriting grows larger and larger,
increasingly illegible, maddening. Shut out of the letters,
left sitting there, Sylvia becomes oppressed by the shelves

and rankings of compulsively ordered history, by the books pressing in from four walls. Feels the disapproving, minatory gaze of the librarian as she bends over each letter, delicately unfolding the onionskin pages, turning them over. The woman, she is certain, is monitoring her breath, the subtlest movements of her fingertips, reading her terrible, shallow thoughts. To spite her, she spends another dutiful hour or so copying comprehensible bits from the letters into her black moleskin journal, until she grows sleepy, heavy, as if Vernon's sloppy inked words were a poison of hemlock creeping through her limbs. Vaguely humiliated that she cannot decipher these letters (not her fault, Vernon's atrocious, broken cursive!), she is convinced the librarian is gloating over her failure. From across the empty, silent room, she feels the woman's disdain. Grating her chair backward, standing up, Sylvia carries the folders over to the librarian, who takes them without a word.

To get down the stairs and back out to the street, Sylvia must walk through a large room adjacent to the library. The room contains a temporary exhibit on the life of a mid-twentieth-century Italian playwright she has never heard of. Enlarged black-and-white photographs of the playwright dominate the walls. A bald, sloe-eyed man, nothing distinctive about him beyond his flaccid face and black beret, his having once been alive. A recording of the playwright's voice, solipsistic and sly, loops endlessly through the empty room.

Crossing via Maggio, Sylvia slips down a narrow passage between buildings. Aside from a man in blue overalls cycling past, she is the only person in the alley. The first time she and Philip had come to Florence, they had visited Leo Giuliano's paper studio on the recommendation of Cesare Lumachelli's wife, Jean, and purchased several of his leather-bound, marbled paper books. She had returned by herself twice more, and on each of those occasions, Leo had stood on a ladder, gotten a scrapbook down off of a high shelf, and leafed through pages of old photos, showing her a younger, handsomer black-and-white version of himself, smiling beside famous people who had once commissioned his work—here, he pointed out, was the Japanese emperor, here, Pope John Paul II and the British queen. After the scrapbook, he took her into his private workroom to show her his family's centuries-old paper marbling technique. Those visits with Leo were among her favorite memories of Florence. Searching now for his familiar shop window, anticipating her first glimpse of him seated at his worktable, hoping he will remember her, she thinks perhaps she might take him to lunch. When she does find the shop, it is shuttered, closed. Padlocked. His name, Leonardo Giuliano, removed from the door.

Of course. In a city haunted and dominated by its dead, people grew old, people got sick. Leonardo had looked unusually tired last summer, had even apologized for being unwell. She had noted the dark-smudged, pouched circles under his eyes, the heavy sighs that gave no relief. She couldn't begin to find his home or ask someone where he lived or who his wife might be. She is a tourist, and this once-famous artisan whom she had imagined her friend is gone, perhaps dead. There is nothing to do but keep walking. At the end of the alley, she squeezes through a turnstile meant to keep cars from entering and finds herself on via Romano, across from that ponderous dark gold fortress, Palazzo Pitti.

Climbing flights of gray marble stairs, stopping several times to catch her breath, she reaches the floor housing the museum's current exhibit, "Florentine Artifacts, Stolen and Recovered." Thinks of Vernon's book in her purse, the one by Jules Romains, an artifact stolen from the British Institute.

Sylvia is the only visitor wandering the sepulchral, climate-controlled rooms, passing recovered artifacts in dim-lit glass display cases. Each palatial room has carved gilt moldings, ceiling murals, wall frescoes. She finds the rooms more interesting than the stories of theft and recovery. Why is she the only visitor? It is June; there should be throngs of tourists.

Her ticket includes the permanent exhibits, but visiting these, too, proves an unsettling experience. Hardly any people are walking along the wide, windowed corridors of the Palatine Gallery, exiting one room, entering another. Museum guards in dingy white dress shirts and black pants sit on black plastic chairs by the doorways of each gallery, each room, the only sound that of humidifiers discreetly monitoring moisture in the air. The guards imitate death by their own silence, heavy stillness. Sylvia walks along immense formal corridors, drapes of gold richly framing floor-to-ceiling windows, conscious of the almost vulgar squeaking of her shoes.

In gallery after gallery, just as she passes through one doorway, someone is leaving through another. Unbelievably, she can stand as close as she wants to paintings by

Raphael, Titian, Rubens, Correggio, works from the Medicis' original collection. Ruskin, James, Wilde, Hawthorne, Dostoyevsky, Eliot, the Brownings, Wharton, Berenson, Pater, Sargent . . . Mary Robinson, Vernon, Kit Anstruther-Thomson—all of them once stood where she is now. The litany unfurls out of sense and sequence, names shuffled out of time. Had there been a single visitor in the gallery besides herself, she could not have received the sensation, palpable, that they are somehow with her, crowding in, spectral, murmuring, filling the room.

Almost finished touring the palazzo's right wing, she finds the Royal Apartments, a series of rooms telescoping into one another, restored from the time they housed the Medici family in the sixteenth century up through the residence of King Vittorio Emmanuel II in the nineteenth. (She has read the plaque on the wall.) Tired of facts, weary of untouchable opulence, Sylvia takes in a last, blurred impression of jade green silk, gold brocade, gigantic carved beds—and clocks. Gilt clocks, enameled clocks, ivory clocks, wood clocks with gold inlay, all run down, impotent, still.

Emerging from Palazzo Pitti, Sylvia feels stunned, assaulted by the harsh late-afternoon glare. Vernon would have walked on this street, possibly with her walking cloak and black bowler, with cropped hair and glasses, her equine face with its long, protruding lower jaw, the glittering eyes. She thinks how nothing in that disarranged face would attract any glance other than one of startled revulsion, tempered, perhaps, with pity. But Vernon's voice, the magnificent mind behind the voice, would be impossible to ignore, would be seductive and, to a few women, irresistible.

Crossing the Ponte Vecchio, which, unlike the deserted Palazzo Pitti, is densely packed with tourists, Sylvia finds a café in the open-air courtyard of Palazzo Strozzi, orders a glass of white wine. She is relieved to be off the streets, away from cars, motorcycles, people talking in loud, careless voices. Especially after Gabinetto Vieusseux and Palazzo Pitti, the world feels too vibrant, fast, insultingly alive.

The chilled wine slips down her throat. At the table nearest her, an Italian man, perhaps in his fifties, heavyset and dressed in a wheat-colored linen suit, sketches something in a large notebook. Suddenly, he sighs, lays down his pen, and with a sad, ceremonial gesture flings the last bit of wine from his glass over one shoulder, then gathers up his things and is gone. From another era, she thinks, another decade. The 1950s. *La dolce vita.*

Again, only the young seem unburdened, always in groups or pairs or, like the two who have just seated themselves on a bench nearby, lovers, openly kissing for what seems to Sylvia an unimaginably long, even unpleasant, time. Is it because their portion of hope has not yet been exhausted, not even been tested? At the same table where the Italian man (or ghost) had sat drawing, an older, well-dressed Italian couple now sit down. The woman carefully arranges half a dozen expensive-looking shopping bags around her feet while the man orders for them: "*Due Campari e due panini, per favore.*" They hold hands, lean in close, taking sensual ease in each other's company. Sylvia imagines them speaking of children, grandchildren, of property, shared history, an intimate prosperity. Hardly ghosts.

There had been an afternoon last summer when she visited her friend Cesare Lumachelli, the translator of two of her earliest novels. They had had a leisurely lunch, then had begun to walk toward his apartment on Piazza dell'Indipendenza, the same building William James had once lived in. Cesare had been born in this apartment, raised his children in the same rooms he had been a child in, nursed his dying mother and father in those rooms. He had lived his whole life in one large, elegant apartment and would likely, either before or after his wife, Jean, die there. Sylvia did not know Cesare's precise age and wouldn't ask, but she guessed he was in his early seventies. "What is it like," she suddenly did ask as they walked, "to have lived your whole life in Florence, where so much has changed? When you walk down the streets you knew first as a child, then as a young man, what is it like for you now? Are your memories layered under the present? Will you share with me what you see, how your memories surface?" For the rest of that afternoon, Cesare shared with Sylvia his memories of the streets they walked on. This would be one of her most intimate memories of their friendship. At one point, he bitterly decried the yearlong occupation of his city by the Nazis, then, as if to cheer himself up, took her into a small pastry shop, where they stood at the counter drinking espresso, eating the pastries he had loved as a boy, pink-iced confections shaped like women's breasts, cloyingly sweet on the first bite, softening into a comparatively bitter chestnut taste. After that, he took her to Biblioteca Marucelliana, a library filled with manuscripts and books from the fourteenth century, a place where university students came to study at long desks, surrounded by rare and gorgeous books from other centuries. As a young man, he told her, he had studied many hours in this library. Some things, at least, had not changed. Then they were back on via Cavour, moving down a side street, heading toward his apartment. "It's true, I no longer understand this place," he said. "Until recently, the souvenir shops run by the Chinese were not here. And the way everyone dresses now, young girls especially, with no modesty, no style, in tank tops, shorts, flip-flops. I risk sounding old-fashioned, but there is no elegance left in my city." Sylvia heard only detachment in his voice, nothing more. "I have outlived my time, that is all, *cara*." "But your novel?" she asked. She knew he had been working on a book for years now. He sighed. "On my desk, unfinished. I still have so many translations to do. Translations pay bills, and we have medical bills now."

She had always considered Cesare a worldly man, a charming cynic—certainly not someone with any investment in theology or spirituality, but to her surprise, as they lingered, talking outside of his apartment building, he told her he had been experiencing increasing moments of clairvoyance. His mother had had that gift, he said, and though she died many years ago, he had begun to see her in his apartment. Her spirit. Rather than frightening him, the apparition comforted him. "There is another world, and frankly, I am ready to go to it." In the hard slant of late-afternoon light, she could see how much Cesare had aged, that he was indeed old. As they said good-bye and embraced, she realized this might be the last time, or one of the last times, she would ever see him. She walked away, convinced of his imminent death, had felt sad for days afterward. One year later, Cesare is perfectly healthy in London, helping his wife care for her mother, who really is dying.

Making her way to the bus stop, Sylvia passes the brass-studded dark brown doors of Biblioteca Marucelliana, its discreet sign, and remembers the mint-green-and-gold interior of that dead palace of ancient books. Then she is in Piazza San Marco, part of the early-evening crowd waiting for buses. Standing in front of the same pastry shop Cesare had whisked her into last summer, she sees an older woman with brassy hair and neon orange lipstick beckoning half a dozen men to follow her upstairs from the street. The way the men move together, with taut, impersonal eagerness, makes Sylvia wonder if the woman is a prostitute. Suddenly, she cannot bear the idea of the long, slow, crowded bus ride and finds the first empty cab in the queue at a nearby cab stand. Her driver listens impassively to the address, switches on his radio to an Italian rock station. As he turns onto Lungo l'Affrico, she feels such relief when he stops in front of Palmerino's gates, she overpays him, doesn't care. Saying nothing, he takes her money, drives off.

The path back to the villa is bordered by pale blue and peach irises, climbing pink roses, and fragrant half-wild hedges of rosemary. Beneath the pergola, on one of the large tables with its dirty beige oilcloth, is a bisque-colored bowl heaped with string beans, ropy, dusty green, still sun-warmed. A second bowl of dark blue ceramic is heaped with orchard plums, and the seam of one overripe plum has burst. Snared in its fibrous golden meat, a wasp struggles, perishing by degrees, of sweetness.

Slipping off her heels, holding them in one hand, Sylvia climbs the stone stairs to her room, changes into loose pants, slips on the familiar shapeless black sweater. Sitting on the edge of the bed, she draws the Jules Romains book out from the bottom of her purse, opens it. On the title page, Vernon's handwriting, a scraggily penciled "February 1935." A few sentences in the book are underscored with the same wavering pencil, and there are several annotations, illegible, not from haste or impatience of temperament, but from age, illness. Sylvia closes the book, holds it in her hands, tries to "feel" Vernon's presence—to feel that night in February, feel what it was like to die and die alone. Feels nothing.

Downstairs, she prepares and eats a light supper of garden spinach and fettuccine, goes back upstairs to work. She has not yet come to that moment when Vernon arrives in Scotland, at Charleton House, and finds herself infatuated with Kit Anstruther-Thomson. Before that can happen, she has to imagine and describe the shame, the catastrophe, with Mary.

Sussex Cottage, Charleton House, and Venice

Sussex
England
July 1882

Vernon and Mary have spent most of the afternoon beneath a blowing green canopy of chestnut trees, Vernon failing to concentrate on a book, Mary fretting over an idea for a new poem, when Vernon spots the calf, broken away from its mother on the opposite creek bank, regarding them steadily with its great black eyes.

She ventures one *Mooo*, then another. The calf stares back, unperturbed, while Mary, flipping her slate pencil in the air, defeated by her muse, rolls onto her back, arms stretched overhead, both legs thrumming a light tattoo on the blanket. After a luxuriant stretch, followed by a blissful sigh, she closes her eyes, reaches over to clasp Vernon's hand.

This is their second summer visiting the Sussex cottage, their last afternoon before returning to London in the morning. Vernon, who plans to stay with several friends before returning to Florence, has given up hope that her passion for Mary will ever be reciprocated by anything other than the chaste mildness and sanguine cheerfulness that Mary seems to possess in endless, irritating quantities. Over the past two weeks, she has shown no variation in temperament, no reaching toward any deeper or different affection between them.

With her hand still in Vernon's, Mary drifts into a light, contented sleep. Placing a narrow black ribbon along the latest page she has failed to read, Vernon closes her book and gazes down at Mary, nudging closer, nestling her head more comfortably in her friend's lap.

"Darling. Darling V," Mary murmurs, eyes closed.

Vernon takes no notice of the lowering skies, of the sharp, short gusts of wind beginning to surge through the chestnut leaves above their heads, the leaves of the oak grove across the creek, the shimmering leaves of the tall bright green poplars lining both sides of the dirt road back to the cottage. Takes little notice of the drop in temperature, the storm's approach, because nothing matters more than this sudden confusion, this racing of her own heart. Mary's face is so close; Vernon studies the black curving lashes, the high, flawless cheek. *Darling. Darling V.* Some fresh, mad hope knocks sense out of her. Has Mary, in some coy, indirect way, just declared an altered affection? She stares at Mary's lips, ripely full, imagines the warm pressure of those lips on hers, the even white teeth, the small tongue. As if sensing herself too closely observed, Mary wakes. The eye not turned blindly into Vernon's lap, blinks up at her.

Devoid of expression, like the eye of a bird or fish, it gazes directly, indifferently, at Vernon.

Thunder rumbles overhead. Across the creek, the sky has gone deep aubergine; the cattle have knotted tightly beneath the oaks, while the calf, motionless, keeps its gaze turned, as if stupefied, in their direction.

Mary separates from Vernon in a single languid movement, sits, and shakes out her full, loose hair. "Only the miller and the baker, quarreling in heaven, isn't that what you always tell me, Vernon dear? How your childhood nurse soothed you?" Lightning jigs silver above the oak grove, and the calf, anxious now, trots at an ungainly pace to find its mother amid the herd's dull bunching in the greenish gloom. Standing, putting both hands to the small of her back, Mary leans back a little before beginning, with her customary alacrity, to gather up their picnic dishes and tumblers, to wrap the leftover plum cake in a towel and empty the dregs from their bottles of ginger beer, to put everything neatly back into the large basket. It is a short walk down the poplar-lined dirt lane to their cottage, and already the first sullen drops of rain have begun to patter against the dusty tops of the chestnut trees. Watching Mary at her practical labors, Vernon thinks that any opportunity for intimacy, if there was one, has passed. Mary remains unvaried in her calm temper, while Vernon's desire rises, crests, threatens to spill over. She forces herself to stand, brush bits of grass and dirt from her pants as the rain, forceful now, penetrates the dense interlacing of branches and leaves. A crack of lightning hits close, as if splitting the sky, and rain falls harder. Mary spins in a slow circle beneath the trees, arms outstretched, face upturned. "Lovely, *chérie*—such lovely rain!" Her musical voice, her laughter are cut off by a sudden sheeting of hailstones pelting down, bouncing off the ground, vibrating from the forceful impact as they hit. The air around them is freezing. Mary kneels, scoops up a handful of the blue-white stones. With her eyes upturned to Vernon's, her dark hair sparkling with rain, Mary slowly opens her mouth, sets a single ice stone on her tongue, shuts her eyes, savoring its cold roundness. Opening her eyes, standing up now, she plucks the hailstone from the warmth of her mouth and offers it to Vernon, who steps close. With the solemnity of a priestess, Mary places the ice on her friend's tongue. But as she steps back, Mary sees it, Vernon's look, not of simple affection, but of helpless longing—no, worse than longing, a look of rank lust on her face. As the slow, awful understanding overtakes Mary's own features, pity (how well Vernon knows that look) mixes with revulsion (that look, too), and a violent new burst of hail shells the earth around them, the noise deafening as Mary drops to her knees and, despairingly (as melodramatic as the weather, Vernon will later think), hides her face in her hands.

The storm abates within minutes, and as soon as the rain has completely stopped, both young women emerge from under the chestnut trees, stepping around great shallow pools of rain, carrying the picnic basket, anchor and barrier between them, up the muddy lane to the cottage. Vernon retires to her room to sleep by herself that last night, while Mary sits a long while in the kitchen, shocked by an awareness that has shamed them both.

In the morning, they go about simple tasks, then close up and leave the cottage, their speech (it could not be called conversation) spare, gelid, polite. What had transpired the day before, been revealed to Mary during the storm, is not broached or spoken of, though it is the one subject between them. The hired coach takes Mary to her parents' new home on Earl's Terrace in Kensington, then delivers Vernon to her friend Bella Duffy's home nearby. After visiting Bella in Kensington, Vernon will stay with another friend, Lady Welby, and from there travel to Muir MacKenzie's home in Surrey, where she will write to her mother and brother that she has just met "the most handsome creature, picturesque really, a half-painter, half-sculptor who dresses 'crane' and rather fast, drives tandem and plays polo. Clementina Anstruther-Thomson, or 'Kit,' as she likes to be called, is a reckless, slangy girl who stammers all over the place. I find I like her very much. She has absolutely worked to persuade me to visit her home at St. Andrews once I leave off seeing the Paters in London, and I have just answered her that yes, I will."

Charleton House
Fifeshire, Scotland
August 1882

The humiliating business with Mary, the strain of visiting too many friends in homes with unfamiliar persons and routines has left Vernon exhausted. On the train to Scotland, she had hoped to recover, to feel a bit better than she does. She waits on the station's platform, first weary, then astonished, as Kit, sporting outlandish driving goggles, a leather cap, and a fur coat, drives up in a modern open-air car spewing high rooster tails of dust. With Vernon in the passenger seat, clamping her felt traveling hat to her head with both hands, she attempts shouting replies to Kit's rapid-fire questions, only to have the wind carry off her words or be drowned out by Kit's maniacal tootling of the car horn every time she whizzes past a horse-drawn coach or hay wagon bumping along the serene tree-lined road leading to the Anstruther-Thomson's ancestral estate. The visit already feels to Vernon like a mistake, yet within a few short hours, her early dread will be reversed.

Dearest Mamma and Eugene,

About Clementina, or "Kit," my new Scottish friend—she strides about the place in tall equestri-enne boots, jodhpurs, ill-fitting men's shirts. Like her affable father, she proclaims her prime passion is riding to the hunt. After a rough, jolting arrival by motor car, I find, thus far, I like her enormously. . . .

After her first dinner at Charleton House, Vernon falls straight asleep, letter unfinished, dreaming of this coltish girl with her tumbled russet hair and direct gaze, her rangy way of flinging herself, loose-limbed, over all the furniture.

The next morning, Vernon follows Kit to the horse stables, and afterward, she will always recall that first strong, not unpleasant impression of horse smells. The pungent, acidic odor rising from rank, spreading pools of urine, milder odors from scattered cobbles of dung, the smell of

leather hunt saddles and rows of tack rubbed soft with lin-
seed oil, the medicinal smell of horse liniments, the field
smell of bran mash, and everywhere the pervasive stink of
horse sweat and, later, outside, the musky scent of sweat
half-mooned beneath Kit's arms as she lunges one of her
stallions in the field. (More than once while she is a guest at
Charleton, Vernon will write certain sympathetic friends,
extolling Kit's bodily genius, sounding besotted, calling Kit
a "living Venus de Milo.")

On the third day of her stay, when the morning's mail
is carried up to her room on a silver tray, the ecru edge of a
small envelope peeks from beneath Eugene's characteristically thick letter, transcribed by Matilda and predictable in
its bombast and neediness. The horrible shock contained
in the scrap of note sent by Mary Robinson will be hinted
at, glanced upon, in one scarcely legible line to her mother,
written that night: "My travel plans are shattered due to an
astonishing occurrence I cannot yet explain."

Five days of silence follow before Matilda receives a second, explanatory letter from her daughter. It seems Mary
Robinson had written to Vernon on that torn scrap of paper
mainly to announce her engagement to a Professor James
Darmesteter of the College of France. Wounding shock.
Devastation. No words. Vernon has since heard from Monica, Mary's sister (the entire Robinson family is in an uproar
of disapproval), that it was Mary herself who proposed this
marriage to Mr. Darmesteter, after meeting him only three
times! More catastrophic still, the professor is crippled and
hideously deformed, a dwarf, a grotesque. Vernon recalled
meeting him once in London—Darmesteter is known to be

a respected scholar, kindly natured, but *marriage* to a man of such extreme defect? Mary has gone mad. In her letter to her mother, Vernon ends one scribbled page of outburst only to begin another, writing how she first received the news, with utter shock, followed by incredulity—is this a joke?—and that now she grows dully resigned. She ends the letter by saying how grateful she is to be "picked up" by the simple, good presence of this rare creature, Kit—who talks as slangily and heedlessly as a schoolboy, cares passionately for trees and grass, animals and painting—for Browning and Shelley, too—and is gravely curious about what is right and wrong and why. . . .

Matilda shrugs off the letter's final, fawning emphasis on someone named Kit as proof of Violet's poorly disguised attempt to ignore the pain of Mary's decision. Mary, whom they have all dearly loved, practically considered a blood relation of the family.

But Matilda is mistaken. Vernon has intentionally left a great many things out of her letter. She does not confide that on the night she received news of Mary's engagement, she had found a white rose, pristine, lushly scented, and cool, on her pillow. (A rose Vernon will preserve between the pages of her Commonplace Book, keeping that book close when, in an attempt at reconciliation, she will go to see Mary in Venice, a book she will keep close when she returns, with Mary, to Florence, only to endure Eugene's cruel remarks regarding the perversity of Mary's choice in husbands, a book she will keep beside her on the day Mary weds Mr. Darmesteter. For the rest of her life, Vernon will keep Kit's white rose preserved between the pages of that Commonplace Book, eventually sealing it in an envelope upon which she will write *"Neue Liebe, neues Leben,"* or new love, new life.)

In subsequent letters to Matilda, Vernon also does not mention how Kit does nothing to damp her infatuation and everything to encourage it. Does not describe the way generations of Scottish privilege, wealth, and rank seem to have bred this creature of indulged temperament, grand-hearted, forever hurtling about in a pair of tight jodhpurs, high black riding boots, badly fitting men's shirts, or galloping downstairs for eight o'clock dinner dressed in that odd new fashion inspired by Walter Crane, short petticoats, which on Kit's tall, athletic body look endearingly ridiculous. Does not linger over any description of Kit's features, boyishly perfect straight on, proud in profile. Does not mention how she can be laconic for most of a day, then suddenly stammer out a jumbled mix of slang and refined sentences, thoughts rushing out, unedited, impetuous, clever. Does not write that Kit is an immense earthly relief from London's drawing room atmosphere, snobbish, vain, taut with condescension.

"Kit is easeful to me," is all she does write to her mother, before proceeding to tramp beaten ground: to think it was Mary!—in a rut of incredulity, she goes over and over this one fact, scrawling across so many pages, she then must cross-write half of them—to think it was Mary who proposed marriage to Darmesteter. All Mary's notion! More unthinkable, the pitiable creature had accepted! She still remembers, from the one occasion she met him, how he had had to crawl across the floor to get to the other side of the room ... though by queer compensation, the man is possessed of a massive intelligence. Everyone in London who knows Mary, who has heard the news, is appalled, repulsed. To throw away such beauty when she is courted by numerous well-set-up men (all while remaining loyal, until recently, in her affection for Vernon) is distressing enough, but to bind herself legally and *eternally* to this monstrous error of nature, to possibly conceive a child with such a malformation, a child who could well prove to be a grotesque copy of its father, is unconceivable, positively suicidal. For days, such letters fly from Vernon's hand to her mother, who opens and scarcely reads them—repetitive tirades—while Kit, hour by faithful hour, is never far from Vernon's side.

Even as she feels Mary's betrayal, Vernon falls more deeply in love with Kit. Watching her rein in a spirited horse, ride to the hunt with Charleton's sleek pack of spotted hounds, take her best Thoroughbred mare over hedges and creeks with ease, heedless of danger. And later, watching her pen hasty, passionate notes to this person or that with the agile hands that control a horse. In comparison to this vital, animal-smelling creature in too-short petticoats, lounging about like a young prince, booted legs crossed, hands behind her head, Vernon feels as fragile as Murano glass. After years of serving her brother, Eugene, then looking after Mary, here is Kit, like some heartsick Scottish lord, kneeling before Vernon, attending to her every desire and adjusting to her every mood, all while declaring she must soon show Vernon how to ride—and why not have her own horse one day? Why not drive a car? Kit can teach her that, too—and why shouldn't the two of them bicycle across all of Italy, fling themselves beneath the natural shelter of trees by night, two brigands in woolen capes, breath intermingling, why not, why ever not?

Over the last year, I have met remarkable women!
The social activist in black, who creates schools for
poor girls. The playwright in her paper gown of blue,
an ethereal shepherdess who speaks in a fey, musical
whisper. The poetess in her long cape of white shells
from the sea, trimmed with bits of poems and green
moss. The opera diva from Venice, powdered and
imperious in scarlet velvet, indifferent to her worship-
pers. And Mary. Is that friendship—that love—gone?
And now, Clementina Anstruther-Thomson. Kit.
I cannot stop thinking of her. I do not care to stop
dreaming of her. The sculpted and still majesty of a
Greek goddess is as nothing compared to her one life.
I love her, I swear it.
                    —from Vernon's 1882 Commonplace Book

To distract Vernon from her pain over Mary, Kit suggests they travel to Lerici, a fishing village in La Spezia. They spend one night in the forlorn cottage next to Percy Bysshe Shelley's Casa Magni, now a dank, deserted place, its walls stained, battered by the same waves, the same sea young Shelley drowned in. Vernon falls ill, and a doctor in Lerici warns them against further travel. Ignoring him, they go on to England, where Vernon suffers a complete breakdown. Dispirited, they return to Charleton House, where Kit nurses Vernon. By March, feeling better, Vernon writes her mother, begging her to move, to find a home in the hills above Florence. She can no longer bear the noise and congestion of the city. "You must find me such a place. I am ill. I am so very ill, Mother. It is desperate. Why, why will you not understand?"

While she implores her mother to find a place in the country, Mary Robinson and James Darmesteter are quietly wed in London.

Vernon grows so much stronger, she and Kit again attempt travel, this time to Tangiers, then Spain, Naples, Rome. But Vernon is depressed in spirit and sees little good in anything; even Kit falls ill, so the trip, for both of them, is a disappointment. Hearing her mother has succeeded in renting a villa in the hills above Florence, she agrees to return home, with Kit promising to follow. But first, Vernon makes plans to meet Mary, now Mrs. James Darmesteter, in Venice. Kit has advised this, urging her to behave kindly toward Mary, to see what might be salvaged. Even if things appear irrevocably ruined, a reconciliation, Kit is convinced, will heal Vernon.

She has scarcely left Charleton House for Venice when she receives Kit's first letter, followed by others, one, sometimes two letters in a day. Dense passages, hurtling along, Kit's prose a perfect mimicry of her high-spirited, natural speech, down to the ink careering across page after page at an upward slant. With vigor, she declares how hungry she is for Vernon's intelligence, eager to submit her poor thoughts for Vernon's critique, ravenous for the gift of books Vernon sends her, the most recent Baudelaire, Flaubert, and her favorite, Rimbaud.

Accustomed to cowing, offending, intimidating, to being the plain-carved queen upon the chessboard, dwarfing smaller, daunted figures, Vernon is undone by these ardent, artless letters. She reads and rereads them.

One does not relinquish love easily. Even an unhappy love. Beneath the portico facing Piazza San Marco, from the screen of a marble pillar, Vernon observes Mary crossing the rain-polished square, a slight, solitary figure in a long walking coat, her open black umbrella buffeted by wind. How small she is. Vernon had forgotten. Mary seems nervous, cloistered by some preoccupation. When a dozen Gypsy children surround Mary, begging, a sadly familiar scenario in Venice, Vernon imagines writing *una fiaba*, a fairy tale, in which the hundreds of pigeons blanketing Piazza San Marco are really the souls of dead Gypsy children. When a person as lovely and kind, as nearly perfect, as Mary appears, the birds briefly take on human form. Afflicted by a dozen such imaginings in a single hour, Vernon dismisses this fantasy even as she makes no move to go to Mary's aid. Mary needs no help. Balancing her open umbrella with one hand, her book satchel with the other, she bends down to speak to the children, who obediently follow her gaze straight up to the twin marble lions guarding the cathedral of San Marco. Whatever she is telling them has them spellbound. When they finally tear their gaze away, when the story she has told them ends, Mary has a coin ready for each one. As the children scatter away, no doubt to find their next mark, Vernon thinks, and with no small ache (having witnessed Mary's charity, she is once again in love with her), no, she will not write some sentimental tale of dead Gypsy children and fat, fluttering, overfed pigeons. Instead, she will stand among spoiled Venetian pigeons strutting and pecking for crumbs near her damp booted feet outside Florian's Café and wait.

As Mary swiftly crosses the last length of the storm-lashed piazza, her head is bowed. Could she be apprehensive at the prospect of meeting Vernon? They have not seen each other since that awful day in Sussex, since Mary's sudden insane engagement and marriage to Mr. Darmesteter. As Mary draws near, raises her face, the strain on it is shocking. Has this awful matrimony proved too great a trial, a foolish impulse Mary already regrets? Energized by the thought, Vernon steps from behind the pillar to greet Mary. Calmly, too calmly, Mary shakes out her umbrella, furls it, and, when Vernon insists on embracing her, shrinks away. Too late. Arousal floods through Vernon, undoing her vow to be solicitous, high-minded. Her body is disobedient, aflame. Even the tips of her breasts burn. She somehow manages to usher Mary into the warmth and amber glow of Flori-an's, request a quiet table near the back. She assumes they will spend most of the afternoon here, warily approaching, then discussing, the one person causing them distress—the foremost person in either of their minds—Professor Darm-esteter. That Vernon still cherishes some slender, secret hope of breaking Darmesteter's hold on Mary is part of the charged, tense atmosphere around the two women.

Florian's is empty, devoid of its gaiety, an effect of the day's grim weather. Seated on delicate chairs of red velvet, surrounded by gilt mirrors, a full silver service with plates of gold-trimmed Wedgewood between them, Vernon and

Mary hardly notice their cups of hot chocolate filigreed with whipped cream, the glacé chestnut macaroons, finger sandwiches, and tiny fruit tarts arranged on a tiered silver dish. Beside her plate of untouched food, Mary's black crocheted gloves lie across one another, like passive, mute creatures. As the two women edge past superficial niceties of conversation, Vernon struggling to accept Mary's decision to marry, Mary assuring Vernon she and James plan on having no children, Mary states plainly that they intend no relations of "any nature" that might risk producing a child. Theirs, she says, looking gravely at Vernon, is a platonic union.

"I consider myself James's disciple," Mary goes on. "I have told him as much. The moment we met, I understood it was my destiny, my fate, to marry him. That is why I proposed. He would never have dared to propose to me or to anyone. He is far too conscious of his deficiencies as a man. You must believe me, Vernon. I could not be happier. I could not feel more right about my life as Mrs. Darmesteter."

Vernon, who will write to her mother later that evening, *"It is plain Mary would die for this man,"* cannot bring herself to look Mary in the eye as she asks the next question, not even as Mary calmly answers.

"That he is so ill-formed, as you say, so very hideous-looking? How do I bear it? My answer is that I do not see the man, the 'creature' you describe. When I look at my husband, I behold only a great soul." She leans across the table, seizes Vernon's hands, and presses them imploringly. "Dearest Vernon, don't you see? I have given myself complete freedom to choose whom I wish to love. And you and I? Since Sussex, we both know all is greatly changed between us. James is my life now. My present and my future. If only you, who were once and perhaps still are, my closest, dearest friend, can accept and understand James and me, grasp the higher purpose of our union, then I should not care if the whole rest of the world disdained and abandoned me, which, I'm afraid, it mostly has. . . ."

Mary's beautifully even features, her white hands, childlike, the fingers pink at their tips . . . all at once Vernon feels Mary's unhappiness, her particular suffering, as her own. With Kit's latest letter hidden in her coat pocket, whimsical miniature sketches leaping off the margins of the pages, with that consolation imparting strength to her, Vernon presses Mary's hands in hers with surprising, loving warmth. "Whatever I do not understand in all of this, darling Mary, I shall learn to understand. You must never apologize to me. It is I who have been unkind in my judgment, I who must apologize to you."

With that, the reconciliation is accomplished. Vernon relinquishes Mary to Mr. James Darmesteter. And if the letting go of Mary is not half as wrenching as she had expected, it has much to do with the delightful love letter in her pocket, written in Kit's coltish, impetuous hand:

> *Bien chere V, most dear little Vernon, thank you so very, very, very much for the Baudelaire! What a duck you are to send me such beautiful things, the charm of them has caught me like a spider in its web, and I just can't put the book down once I open it . . . if I try to think my thoughts about Baudelaire—he makes me*

waste all my time when I am indoors!—they just go
bang out of my head. It must be a woe to you to have
such an illiterate friend as yours beaucoup beaucoup.
Oh, Arthur says "Miss Paget is too adorable, give her
my love" . . . (I don't because you have it all). Good
night, nice Vernon, dormez bien. You _feel_ *quite near*
though I suppose a crow would have to fly a long way
to search you. And what pretty things you said to me
before you left _would_ *have turned my head if I* _had_ *a*
head, but not having one, it's still right side up, how's
that *for English? Drop me a wee line, bien à toi, Ver-*
non, chérie. . . . I blow you a kiss, darling.

Mary and Vernon spend four days in Venice. While Mary
does research for her new book of poems, Vernon, wandering the canals, happens upon the funeral ceremony of
a Venetian girl and is moved enough by the experience
to write an essay, "The Bead-Threader's Funeral and the
Church of the Greeks." Over dinner at the hotel that night,
she reads aloud to Mary from the section closest to the end.

"The poor little consumptive maker of bead garlands
for cemeteries is indeed now—save, perhaps, for her
mother—of as little importance as the dead kitten
bobbing up and down, a sleek, grey ball, in the green
waters of her native canal. But that just answers to
the truth. The poor (let us have courage to say it)
leave no trace behind, and are in this respect less of
a fraud than the rich, who possess ancestors with
names, and for their bones, inscriptions and what

the French call concessions à perpétuité—to wit, their measure of earth properly paid for all eternity. There is wonderfully little lux perpetua for any of us; and the poor are too busy and have too little house-room for each individual's addition to the common fund of life, the crowd of living beings, the group of surviving thoughts and emotions, to be labeled with an individual memory. This does not prevent little makers of glass-bead garlands, even when they die of consumption at nineteen, from having played their part—perhaps been happy and made others happy (some nice, clean young fellow like the one who pulled off his red cassock to take an oar)—and being glad that they too will have a funeral service with married friends in black, girl friends in white, wax dips, and fine Latin words promising some vague glory which is, after all, this."

Prepared to read to the end, only a page or so more, while Mary dips a spoon in and out of her broth of rice and salted cod and listens, they are interrupted by an acquaintance wishing to introduce them to the poet Gabriele D'Annunzio, just arrived at the hotel. ". . . ugh, what a terribly yellow little man, thoroughly odd, though he has a book of stories just out, *Terra vergine*," Vernon writes Matilda later that night, "though of course Mary and I have read both his poetry collections, *Primo vere* and *Canto nove*." Casually, as if in afterthought, she adds that she and Mary will arrive on Saturday, in two days' time. "Mamma, do tell

Eugene I insist he not be rude to Mary, nor acidic or outrageous in his opinions. She and I are reconciled, so he absolutely must be civil and decent."

But Eugene, on his catafalque, is morose, his melancholy relieved only by accusation. When Vernon and Mary arrive from Venice, he spares neither of them, expressing withering contempt for Mary's choice of a husband. Vernon tries to shield Mary from him, from Matilda as well, who wishes to explore the philosophical implications of "this unfortunate matter." The moment Mary is safely on an early train to London, Vernon scarcely manages, before taking to her bed, to scratch out this note: "Darling Kit, *venez!* Restore me, *chérie!* . . . ever your V."

V.

⎯⎯∞⎯⎯

*Dead less than a century and I find myself exhumed, roughly
labeled as a jam pot. Bosh. Look how she pores over scholarly
articles, underlining, scribbling in the margins, studies photographs (few enough of those, since I was loath to have my
image reproduced), turns me into black ink on a yellow pad
before changing me into light, fingers flying over her laptop's
keyboard, for hours, days at a time.*

*I observe her through the sly, chatoyant eyes of my cats.
Before the sun rises, I slip through the window she leaves
open, an invitation to touch her auburn hair, her pale, composed features.*

*The question of my sexuality is endlessly debated, specu-
lated upon, by well-intended scholars, all of whom are wrong.
The "promiscuity" of my desire—for, until Kit, I was promis-
cuous in my worship of beautiful women—was nonphysical.
Incorporeal. Even with Mary, my desire was forced to atro-
phy, die. After that terrible last afternoon at the Sussex cottage, I came to fear that a physical kiss would consume me,
a human touch destroy me. I became frightened of sexuality.
Only writing was safe, brought pleasure. I never confessed the*

details of that day to Kit, yet, empathetic soul!—she under-
stood my aversion to touch, tolerated my virginity, even as
she vehemently opposed it. "I am human, Vernon!" she cried
out during our worst quarrel. "I need to be loved as humans
love!"

I move Sylvia's pen, my invisible hand over hers. Page
after page, I help her set down truth, how it was first with
Mary, then Kit. She allows this, does not fear what I often
wrote about when fleshed—the supernatural. White margin
between worlds.

Latin: sylvia.   Italian: della foresta.

French: de la fôret.   German: komme Wald.

Perfect, her name.

Sylvia

IT ISN'T THE SOLITARY WALK to the bus stop or even the bus ride into Florence. She doesn't mind being compressed into stillness among strangers. It is more what she felt the last time, stepping down off the bus in front of the flower shop near Piazza San Marco. That she was somehow outside of the physical world even as people thronged solidly around her. This new loneliness is, strangely, a relief. A relief because she no longer yearns for inclusion, for the warmth of others or another. She moves among Florence's citizens and tourists, people walking or cycling past, as if she were a revenant, a specter, as if she passes right through people and if they feel her at all, it is only as a small current of disturbance. Sylvia's final moments in the city of Florence could best be described as aloof, wistful. Not unbearable, but she will find any further temptation to go into the city unappealing, almost frightening.

If she goes anywhere now, it is to buy a few things at the grocery next to the Shock Café—a store open weekdays from 4:00 to 6:00 P.M. and so tiny, it stocks a minimum of goods. Managed by a fastidious little man in a grocer's jacket, his undeviating response to Sylvia purchasing his food is one of irritated courtesy. Fresh fruit and baguettes, cheese, canned goods, wine and chocolate—she chooses from these. Other times, she takes long walks in the hills, along quiet roads paved and bordered by ancient trees, stone walls, gates of ornate iron design, behind which drowse the great shuttered yellow, gray, rose, or dun villas. The roads feel reserved, cool, oneiric—occasionally a car rounds a curve, announcing its approach with a single muffled honk. Sylvia belongs to the hourless quiet. The old German shepherd, Palma, has begun to follow her on these walks, skulking behind her, sometimes stealing close enough to nudge at her hand with a dry pink-scabbed nose before falling back again. Afraid Palma will be hit by a car, Sylvia stops every few feet to yell at the dog to go home. *"Vai a casa!"* she orders, pointing sternly back toward the villa. Eventually, she gives up, since the dog's response is to hide, almost comically, behind a shrub or a tree until Sylvia resumes walking; then Palma follows suit, following at a determined, stalking trot.

If she tries sneaking out, the gaunt yellow dog still finds and trails her, eerily loyal, parasitic. She has no idea how Palma escapes the villa's walls and locked gates. His persistence is unsettling, as there is no affection or companionship in it. Eventually, she decides she has no option but to let Palma lurk along, and hope there will be no accident, fatal or otherwise.

On the day she meets the astronomer, Sylvia oversleeps. When she finally does wake, her room is rinsed to opaqueness by sunlight, the silence interrupted by a single honeybee, frantically buzzing before finding its way through an open window. Downstairs, she finds familiar evidence of Remo—her coffee, grown cold now, fresh-picked peas in their lumpy green jackets piled in a shallow wooden bowl, the familiar bisque bowl full of more ripe, dusky-skinned plums. He must be out in the vineyards or the garden—his empty coffee cup is in the sink, alongside a plate littered with the remains of his breakfast. The two of them under the same roof—implacably shy, fixed in their polite daily exchanges. Reheating the coffee, she carries her cup upstairs, along with a slice of *focaccia* and a plum, eats, thinks about the writing. But it is so beautiful out, she feels as if she literally cannot sit still, cannot stay inside.

According to certain scholars, a hidden garden exists somewhere on the grounds of Villa il Palmerino, a secluded, gladelike spot Vernon Lee had designed to be secret, impossible to find. This could be the perfect day to search for that garden. She won't take her usual paths, one leading her from the villa to the road, another going up the grassy slope to the clothesline, a third path up to the fenced pasture where she sometimes goes to find the ancient roan mare, shambling out from under the shade of plum trees to snuffle at Sylvia's outstretched flat palm with her silver-whiskered muzzle, nipping up bits of the stale baguette she offers. There is one other footpath she knows she has not yet taken, a path that, according to Remo's gestures and few words when she'd asked, will take her to the "laundry room." Perhaps if she follows that path, she'll come upon Vernon's rumored (and it is only a rumor, as no one seems to have ever found it) garden.

Carrying a small armload of soiled clothing, she comes upon the footpath accidentally—it is so small and unmarked—only when she stoops to retrieve a fallen sock from the gravel path. Following its gentle descent, trying to keep her laundry from snagging on the wild undergrowth, she discovers a half-rotted shed choked with vines, hidden by trees growing close and tight around it. Propped along every outside wall of the shed is a single-file rank of rust-bitten shovels, rakes, hoes with sun-faded, splintering, or broken handles, bits of black rubber hose, old straw brooms, a glittering nest of gigantic teardrop-shaped green glass bottles, thick and handblown, used for the villa's homemade wine. Using her shoulder to push open the shed door, she steps into a windowless, dirt-floored room, dim and smelling of damp leaf mold and rotted humus. A small front-loading washing machine is already in use; beside it, lopsided wood shelves are crammed with white plastic jugs of detergent brightly labeled in pink and blue. Opposite the washer is a tall beige metal cabinet, padlocked. There is a second room, curtained off by thick plastic sheeting. She drops her dirty clothes on top of the washer, waits for it to finish its groaning, juddering cycle. After a few minutes, Sylvia gives in to her curiosity and, with a faint sense of trespass, draws aside the plastic sheeting to peer into the second room. Men's clothing, dark-colored, spills out from a black plastic bag set between two shabby hard-shelled suitcases. A lightweight aluminum clothes rack, empty of clothes, strangely modern, gleams in the semidarkness. Beside the shining rack, a single cane-bottomed chair and, neatly lined up beneath its seat, a pair of cheap sneakers and a pair of old-fashioned black dress shoes. A lightbulb dangles from the raftered ceiling, festooned in spiderwebs. The air is fetid and stinks of mouse droppings, harsh detergent, and mildew. Amid this lonely enterprise of male clothing, propped against one wall, is the broken black umbrella Remo had held protectively above her head the evening she'd arrived. She lets the plastic sheet fall, crackling, back into place.

As the washer spins into its final eruptive cycle, she waits beside it, thinks about Remo. Taking his afternoon nap on Giustina's small blue couch. Making her coffee each morning. Gathering fruit and vegetables from the garden. Working in the vegetable rows. Pushing an empty wheelbarrow uphill. She watched from her window the time his right hip gave way, saw how he had had to take hold of his leg with both hands, literally swing it around to the front to get it working again—as if the socket had collapsed, as if the bone of the socket had deteriorated so badly that there was nothing to hold the joint in any consistent, straightforward motion. She had seen the pain, undisguised, on his face. Yet he never mentioned his leg, never complained, not to her at least. When she'd asked him about it that night, what was wrong with his leg, his hip, he'd answered first with a shrug, then with a few words and gestures, from which she'd surmised something about a doctor in Bologna, a surgery costing too much money, the entire subject seeming to wound him more than the leg itself. He'd chosen to adapt, a stoic, to his suffering. Still, to have witnessed that moment (and surely there were others) when his hip gave way, came unhinged, swung loose, was a terrible thing, terrible to see suffering distort his face while the gold cross on its chain glinted against his sun-browned chest. The caretaker, whose bed is a short, narrow couch in someone else's home, whose few belongings are stored in a dirt-floored shed infested with mice, who tends someone else's land—what do he and Sylvia have in common? Only that they live in the same house, greet each other with exaggerated courtesy, are reined in from deeper conversation by a mutual inability to speak beyond the most basic sayings in each other's languages? She greets Remo every day, watches him from her window, sometimes sensing there is something fated but ineffable between them. They are bound up loosely in each other's daily lives; perhaps that is the destiny, the only mystery, nothing more.

Wearing Giustina's large black sweater, a pair of her loose dark sweatpants, even her too-big walking shoes—Sylvia wears the older woman's clothing all the time now—she pulls Remo's damp, worn-out T-shirts, faded shorts, disintegrating underwear from the washer, puts them in a small white plastic basket, bends down to shove in her own clothing, pour in a laundry powder that smells acrid yet sweet, takes a few frustrating minutes to figure out how the washer works. Hot with the effort, her face flushed, she leaves the shed and heads toward the north side of the villa, hoping to pursue in earnest the possibility of Vernon Lee's hidden garden. Following a new footpath among overgrown trees and half-wild hedges, the unused-looking path snakes through a lemon grove before opening into unobstructed sunlight, where she sees a man on a small shaded patio, sitting and reading a book. The noise she inadvertently makes, stepping out from the grove, causes him to look up from his book, unsurprised at the sight of her. Rising to half his height, he gestures with impeccable, if stooped, courtesy, for her to come over. When she stands on the edge of the patio, he straightens, extends a hand in introduction. "Richard Asquith. You the writer staying at Giustina's place? I've seen you about here and there, not wanted to disturb you. Shall I bring you a glass of water with lemon, or an orange juice?"

Standing there in Giustina's clothing, shoes loose as shells on her feet, her face red, damp with sweat, Sylvia asks for water, mainly so he will disappear for a few minutes into his living space, yet another cave overgrown with vines, hidden among untrimmed trees. Hoping to compose herself a little, she sits down at the outdoor table, its glass surface rain-streaked, littered with leaves, and glances at the book he had been so absorbed in, its pages bound in antique brown leather, its gilt title worn. She leans in, turns the book toward her, lifts up one of its thin pages. The text is in Italian, half the page taken up with a plate engraving of some sort of ancient scientific instrument. She makes out the name Galileo and the word *astronomia* in the title at the top of the page. This must be the reclusive astronomer Natalia had mentioned during Sylvia and Philip's visit last summer. One of the world's leading experts on Galileo. "Richard," she told them, "has lived in the same apartment on our property for years now. He is from Boston, I think, eccentric, brilliant, but a sweet man, very kind."

The astronomer steps out from his apartment holding two glasses of ice water, each with a precisely cut wedge of lemon. For a hermit, he is elegantly dressed in a pressed pale pink oxford-cloth shirt. His fine white hair is impeccably combed. One of those men, she thinks, who ages in an especially poignant way, the face remaining boyish, round-featured, but with deep creases, thick folds. In photos, depending on the light, he might resemble the child he once was, except now he is very old. His eyes, the most unsettling part of his face, are hard for Sylvia to look at. Very large, faded to a sickly watery blue, with lower lids that droop down in half-moons, cuticles of crimson rimming the whites, as though he has gazed too many years into telescopes, pored over too many ancient texts in darkened libraries, been chronically sleepless. His eyes have a look of mild infection, their unnatural pinkness accentuated by his shirt. As he gazes across the glass table at her, raising his water glass in a friendly toast, the permanent fatigue in his eyes is momentarily usurped by a rapt hunger for human intimacy. She raises her glass, takes a sip, her gaze focused on his shirt, pink, pristine, pressed. Years ago, he explains, Giustina turned half of the ground floor of her place into two small apartments. Both are tucked away, so camouflaged by trees and shrubbery that even Sylvia had not guessed anyone lived here, only steps from her own room. The second apartment, he tells her, is rented out by a rather famous German translator of art books. He is in Prague at the moment, doing research. Werner Leipzig—has she heard of him? He then asks perfunctorily about her work; Sylvia's answers are clumsy, vague. She hasn't adjusted to this unexpected rupture in her solitude, and it is obvious that for Richard Asquith, too, showing interest in someone living is an effort, a memory of manners he might once have possessed. But the moment she asks him about his work, mainly to deflect his inquiries about hers, he becomes charged, animated, voluble. He is just back, actually, from a long morning at the library on via Cavour. Does she know the Biblioteca Marucelliana, a library dating from the fifteenth century? An exasperating place. He is waging battle within its sacrosanct pale green walls. "What do you mean by battle?" she asks. He goes into a convoluted explanation about the jealous death grip Italian scholars and scientists keep on Galileo, a Florentine, one of their own. Over the years, as Richard has delved deeper, expanding his findings on Galileo, he has had to seek out increasingly rare texts, and with this a sinister game has ensued, a game of hiding those texts from him, keeping crucial information he needs out of reach, arcane, untouchable. No matter how many letters of reference he produces, no matter how many official permissions he obtains from various governmental agencies, there are always Italian scholars, Italian scientists, in league with Italian librarians, finding fresh ways to thwart him, to stall him, to keep him permanently waiting. Thus he has been here years, as obstinate and patient as they are deceptive and elusive. He can prove none of this, of course, but he knows it is so. This, he adds, is battle as only scholars and scientists can wage it, subtle, vicious, bloodless.

As he talks, leaning in toward her, his obsession closes over him. She sees the fine English broadcloth shirt is frayed at the cuffs, that the tie is rumpled and stained. His breath smells slightly rotten. Something derelict, neglected, almost mad has risen up in him with fast, dismaying intensity. She both does and doesn't want to see how he lives inside his apartment, this man who appears to be as withdrawn from society, as determined to capture some spectral bit of the past, as she is. If the ghost he chases is Galileo, hers is Vernon Lee. Perhaps it is no accident they are both here, secular hermits at Villa il Palmerino, secluded from the world. And the German translator, is he, too, lost inside his research, his creations?

He is talking, unaware she's stopped listening. What was his name? Richard. Yes, Richard. But she had already discarded that name, thinks of him as *l'astronomo*.

"These old Italian libraries, dating back to the Medici, are war zones of paper and ink, full of jealously guarded secrets. I have been kept at arm's length for years by endless requests for letters, forms, required signatures of persons impossible to locate, often deceased. I will wait them all out. Every last one of them. I will not tire or give up and go home. I have no home to go back to. Let them play their infernal game. In time, I will prevail. Or die, hopefully of natural causes, in the attempt." He smiles, and again she is struck by his odd old boyishness. "It sounds more valiant than it is. Day to day, it is monotonous. And terribly, terribly tiring."

Conversation stops as the specter of *l'astronomo*'s death, his work unfinished, his genius thwarted, is raised. He drinks, sucking water down noisily, bangs the empty glass back down on the table, studies her with those awful pink-rimmed but not unkind eyes, and asks if she has been to see the two treasures of the area—Il Cave, a restaurant just up the road from the San Martino monastery, and the Sunday-morning concerts at the Scuola di Musica di Fiesole. Last Sunday's was Mendelssohn.

"I haven't, I'm afraid. I've been so caught up in my work."

Getting to either place, he tells her, involves a healthy walk, but if she enjoys excellent food and classical music, she should try to go to one or both. Plucking a small gold pen and piece of notepaper from his breast pocket, he sketches two sets of directions. She is grateful he does not ask to accompany her. After giving her the little maps, he escorts her the few steps back to the grove she had so recently emerged from. Thanking him for the water, the directions, she feels suddenly overpowered, drugged, by the citrus-blossom scent of the lemon trees. And in that moment, Sylvia finally does look into the astronomer's eyes, past their raw, scoured pinkness, glimpses what he sees, constellations, galaxies, eons of time, the fading infinitesimal print of ancient texts and extinct formulae. No wonder he can barely speak with anyone; he is only at ease gazing into pleiadian universes, crumbling alchemies. Pressing her hand in a courteous gesture, he is saying something, leaning down, speaking to her. He's just received a postcard from Giustina in Kerala. It seems she is not returning to Italy, to Palmerino, for some time. Her guru has asked her to stay on.

"Wouldn't surprise me," he says, gazing up past the lemon grove, his slow, sweeping, watery gaze always finding the sky, "if old G. never came back. India is her home now. How long will you stay on?"

"Another week." Saying this, she realizes this is no longer true. With Giustina away, she could probably stay on longer, as long as she likes. But who would she become if she did? She is already so alone, increasingly careless of her appearance. Eccentric. Still, a sudden, stark joy comes over her at the thought that she doesn't have to leave.

"You are in her room, aren't you, in G.'s upstairs bed-room?" He is staring at the black sweater, the shoes, both clearly too big for Sylvia, trying to place where he may have seen them before.

He presses her hand again, turns in relief back to his books, his private world. Well, she thinks, she has found a neighbor as strange or stranger than herself. She had enjoyed speaking English with another American, but now, like the astronomer and his stars, she longs for Vernon's presence, for the unnumbered pages piling up with increas-ing abandon around her. Longs for the feeling of her pen, dragging her along, for the voice she sometimes "hears" with such piercing clarity, it hurts. This book is unlike any she has ever written before. She wonders if it is even she who is writing it. Considers it likely she is being helped by someone immaterial, someone she cannot see.

Suddenly hungry, Sylvia goes into the kitchen. The back door has been left wide open, letting in a number of buzzing, lethargic flies. Brushing one especially plump, sluggish fly off an unwashed plate with several broken, stale biscuits on it, she watches it circle back, obdurate, to land on the same plate. She pours a glass of garnet-col-ored wine, not Villa il Palmerino's, opens the refrigerator, breaks off an ivory hunk of Parmesan cheese, plucks two of the ripest plums from the earthenware bowl and, tak-ing a small baguette of bread, carries everything upstairs, sits at her desk to eat before reviewing what she'd writ-ten, worked on, the day before. Vernon Lee's secret glade, wherever it is, can wait.

Kit

Villa il Palmerino
San Gervasio
April 1886

Setting a green earthenware vase of scarlet anemones beside the bed, she hears the cook below in the kitchen, heavily, rhythmically chopping vegetables in preparation for dinner, attempting to follow the scrawled list Vernon had handed her the night before, a list of eighteenth-century Florentine recipes. Vernon had other orders for her, as well. If the traditional Easter cake, now three days old, is stale, it must be replaced by a rum jelly or, failing that, a blancmange, flavored with almonds, dusted with nutmeg. The servants must carry dinner upstairs to the salon, light a fire in the fireplace, use only Matilda's best dishes and linens. Oh, and everyone must be freshly bathed, cleanly dressed.

This bedroom, Kit's, faces west. A shuttered window overlooks the single road from Florence, a dirt road beaten hard with travel, rutted from storms. Beyond the road are vineyards, rolling hills blanketed in blue mist, and, everywhere this fresh April morning, the cool spring air.

Sounds of a piano drift out from the window of the salon upstairs. Matilda, playing Liszt again. Eugene will be lying near his mother, amassing poetic images that Vernon will no doubt be expected to write down for him. The thought irritates her. Lying down, she turns her gaze to the jar of scentless anemones and wills that a ghost trace of her body, her essence, remain on the bed. She draws Kit's latest letter out of her pocket, unfolds and rereads it.

Beloved little Vernon, I shall be so glad to see your face again, chérie, it feels like a year since I saw you! And what a chivalrous sort of mortal you are! What a tremendous difference you have made to Miss Robinson by being good to her and by aquiesing (how do you spell this word?)—just all the difference in her life, I should imagine. What a kind chap you are, Vernon! You, who are so much to me, more than all the pens and inks of this world could ever tell you! I met H. James the other night, had a long talk by the fire. Well, it's nearly dinnertime, 8-0-0 as usual! So goodbye for the present. If you are still with Miss Robinson, say all the nicest of pretty things to her from me. Tout à toi, I blow you a kiss (though I must tell you I am still loath to give up hunting, as you wish me to! If I give up hunting in this country, I shall lose caste; it's only the fact of my being a good horseman that prevents everyone from disdaining me utterly) . . .

what a crooked, illegible scrawl I am writing you, to be sure, but having <u>begun</u> the day early this morning on a violent sort of horse of my Father's, I am <u>finishing</u> the day very tamely propped up on the sofa with a lot of cushions. It rained hard, I got very tired riding, so I was glad to come home, though I liked some of it (don't shrug your shoulders and call me a fool—it's an homage to my surroundings you know, decidement, besides, I <u>like</u> hunting and everything looked so beautiful). You will be good to me, won't you, ma très chére, in which case nothing else matters much, and now, Vernon, though "You are YOU and I am i," as Browning would say . . . I blow you a kiss goodnight, dearest . . . Kit

> *ps: O—this is what children call "a kiss"*
> *& it is for you.*

Beneath Vernon, downstairs, the cook drops and shatters a dish, counterpoint to the piano keys rippling, undulating beneath her mother's restless white hands, her mercurial fingers sounding Lizst's aural landscape. With her eyes closed, Vernon imagines Kit's journey from Charleton House to Paris, from Paris to Florence's train station near Santa Maria Novella . . . sees her now, perched beside Beppe on the edge of the wagon's wide plank seat, angular, eager, pitched forward as if to reach Vernon sooner, taking in with her wide, active gaze the long rise of road up from the city, the turn onto via Lungo l'Affrico, that deeply shaded road so many have traveled up to visit the Pagets, a winding incline alongside the same gentle stream Boccaccio mentions, with its waterside tatting of green cress and rough-toothed mint, its delicate white and yellow blooms, the road hugging the stream for a long while, then gradually leaving the horse carriages and crowds of Florence behind, the air growing quieter, quieter still, until there is only the mild, desultory rustling of trees, birdsong, the jingle of brass bells on the mules' harnesses. Beppe will come to that last turn, that steepest rise, at the exact moment when Kit first glimpses, on the road's right side, set flush against it, just as Vernon had written—Villa il Palmerino—a two-storied villa, canary yellow, bordered by clay pots vivid and bursting with scarlet geraniums.

When Kit does first see this startling brilliance of bright yellow and red, flashing out from a sun-dappled dark green of trees and vineyards, she cannot envision that she will live here with Vernon, off and on, nearly ten years, and that within this villa, little more than a renovated farmhouse, lives the peculiar family she will come to know well. So well that she will see two of them, first Henry, Vernon's father, followed by Matilda, her mother, from their individual sick-beds to their separate graves. So well that she will also see Vernon's brother, Eugene, resurrected and briefly married. Bumping along in the wagon beside the Pagets' caretaker as he drives the mules toward Villa il Palmerino, she foresees nothing of this, but what she feels—deeply senses—is that proud, drumming heart of Vernon's, beating unevenly now, shaking the whitewashed walls, the stone floors and wood beams of a house centuries old, its rooms holy niches for ancient spirits, spectral scenes invisibly playing out, end-lessly repeating . . . the ghost of the man who built the villa, naming it Palmerino after the palm branches carried back

as souvenirs from the Crusades . . . the ghost of the Medici
jeweler, sketching his subtle designs . . . the ghosts of ton-
sured, brown-robed Cistercians who turned the villa, for a
time, into a cloister. And now, this morning, the bright yellow walls of Villa il Palmerino contain Matilda's capricious
spirit, the father's, too, though isn't he always out-of-doors,
as Vernon has described, and the paralyzed brother, Eugene,
vindictive, saturnine, gifted. And Violet/Vernon Lee—forever writing, writing even in the books she reads. Kit has
often observed and remarked upon it, how V. must always
cramp every margin, every blank space with scribblings,
plumed exclamation points, inky arguments! Kit feels all of
this, leaning forward as if to hurry along the mules, scruffy
taupe beasts, battered straw hats on their heads, long,
twitchy ears poking through, dragging the wagon uphill
with their dumb forward patience, bringing her ever closer
to a place she will come to know, to the family awaiting her,
each of their lives ticking on until that hour when they, too,
turn to ghosts, drifting through rooms, haunting the half-
wild gardens of Palmerino.

Here is space Vernon loves. That liminal pause between
anticipation and occurrence, the pleasurable margin, a
wide, open column she can mentally or actually pen over
with longings, passions, poetry, and song. To prefer that
space, cleave to the margin preceding and following a thing
that occurs. The occurrence itself allowing no room for the
gentlest of desires, whims, speculative fancies, the event
limited to itself. On either side, however, everything imag-
inable is possible.

Is this why Vernon constantly, compulsively writes, each page an oceanic white margin she must turn dark and living, seething with ink? This need to overwrite blankness, much as she now lies on the blankness of a bed that will soon hold Kit. Is this why Vernon wants to leave her impression, scribe her flesh's weight on the bed?

Vernon crosses the room to stand before the long glass, its surface reflecting the vase of scarlet anemones, a bit of shutter, and the blue April sky. She regards herself solemnly. The mirror is not Vernon's friend; it is scarcely an acquaintance. Still, she tries to assess her form objectively, as if studying a work of art or an artifact, trying to come to impartial aesthetic judgment. What would a person, any person, upon first seeing her, think? Feel? The answer is unchanged in both cases. Pity. Pity for ugliness with no solution. Not true, for there is a solution, and Vernon found it long ago. She learned to reject her image, carry on as if flesh were not a visible fact. If her face has no reality to her, she reasoned, it cannot have reality for others. Instead, Vernon's incumbent mind, her gleaming expanse of brain, her voice expressive of that brain, will prove the instruments of forgetting. The instruments, too, of seduction. Rise above the body, rise far, far above, and others may follow, some even to worship.

But it is Clementina Anstruther-Thomson before whom she must one day stand physically naked. Kit who must lend her the courage to be kissed. Opened. Loved.

Lambs' tongues, gray and curling, floating in dark chocolate sauce. Birds' claws, pink and tender, cooked into the runny center of an omelette. Pigeons' feet, to be exact.

"Does *la famiglia* Paget dine like this every evening?" Kit's mouth works calmly, without pause, as though she has supped upon tongue and claw every moment of her life.

"My sister is insane," Eugene replies. He has been tilted up, his dinner spooned into his mouth by the latest valet. "Mad as the moon. I say she carries her obsession for history, for anything especially antique or bizarre, to an extreme when she imposes it upon our dinner and upon our guests. I apologize for Violet's peculiarities."

"But thee liked the blood-orange ice, darling heart. Thee approved the Easter cake, as well," Matilda says, fork aloft, long white ringlets bobbling, old-fashioned, queer-looking, against her rouged cheeks. "Which cake shall be tonight's dessert, presumably."

But yesterday's dove-shaped Easter cake, half-eaten, its wings feathered with sliced, sugared almonds, sits ignored in the kitchen as the cook puts final touches on another impossible antique recipe Vernon has requested she make, a Sicilian rum jelly.

"Sweets are sweets no matter the century." Eugene belches lightly and stops chewing long enough to permit the valet to daub at the corners of his mouth with a large, soiled napkin. "We all crave them."

As Matilda and Kit finish driving dessert spoons through their wobbly, anemic jellies, at last setting them down with plain relief, Vernon scrapes away at the last rummy bits in her bowl while servants clear the table, bearing downstairs the exact dishes they had recently borne up, lighter now. In the salon, it turns gloomily formal, silent, only the clink of bone china and silverware being

collected, while on the other side of the double doors, servants descend the staircase, chattering, one bursting, off-
key, into Puccini's aria "O mio babbino caro." The sound
trails, then vanishes into the kitchen.

Matilda breaks the digestive lull by explaining to Vernon's guest, Clementina, the Paget household routine, if
indeed there could be said to be one.

"We entertain visitors, should visitors arrive, from four
until seven. Often we have no one at all for weeks, then a
dozen souls descend at once as if by natural migration or
Gypsy caravan. Two months ago, Oscar Wilde nearly ran
over William James and his brother Henry on the stairs.
Edith Wharton stopped by twice, just after Rilke's visit, hoping to talk with Vernon, and that strange, dashing Russian
poet—what's his name, Eugene, the one who is so desperately in love with thee? He arrived impromptu, then lingered like an ague for three interminable days. And always,
thanks to Violet, who cultivates them like plants, we have
the Italians, hordes of Italians. She invites them all, artists, critics, poets, translators, and our good neighbors, the
Pasolinis and the Rasponis, of course. And as thee may have
already deduced from his empty seat at dinner this evening,
Henry, my husband, goes largely missing."

"In mind as well as form," Eugene quips, prone again,
eyes fixed on a spot of soot-blackened ceiling.

"*C'est vrai.* Henry is a hunting man. He prefers the out-
of-doors, where animals, not people, live. The fish and the
fowl. Or else he sits at the train station, reading foreign
newspapers and watching people, the strangest animals of
all, come and go. No doubt he saw thee, Clementina, arrive

by train this afternoon, and when thee depart, he will see that, too. When weather permits, we take Eugene for open-air drives in the country. We have a special bed kitted out in the wagon, with a canvas canopy we unfurl over him in case of rain."

"My mother and Violet—like my mother, I refuse to call my sister anything but Violet—insist on my being put out, like some sad potted fern, into fresh air. I accede to their whim, even though I have scarcely more than a worm's-eye view of anything. If it rains, I am granted the false heaven of a canvas roof."

Matilda ignores her son. She will later confess to Kit, who is an easy person to confess to, that he bores her to catatonia. "I do hope thee likes music, Clementina. I play continuously, often at odd hours of the night, whenever I cannot sleep."

"Mother's quite good, actually very good. Though her Chopin is rubbish, and she overplays poor Liszt, who, could he hear her, would spout blood from his grave. She is best with Haydn."

"I thank thee, Eugene, for both the compliment and colorful criticism. Our Violet, as thee must already know, writes incessantly whenever she is not buried up to her failing eyes in books. Books, books, books. My fault, this obsession. On occasion, an urge to garden, to poke about in the same dirt Michelangelo may have walked upon, takes her out of doors. The *uova fragile*, the strawberry grape, one of her more successful grafts. Violet does like to graft things. Dabble in horticulture. Life with my children is an intense exercise. Violet, for instance, insists on quiet, so it becomes too much a medieval cloister or tomb for my taste, but then we have our salons for relief. Less relieving are her *cultes*, all those mannish young women who trot up from the train, alone or in bovine clumps, to grovel at her feet, all the while managing to eat and drink like feral cats. Her appeal to them is enormous. Eugene and I don't understand it."

"Oh, I do," Kit says, still eating, having kept hold of her dinner plate and sawing off yet another cold dib of lamb stewed in cacao. "Vernon—Violet—is roaringly brilliant. Men tend to hate how brilliant she is; she outshines them. Quite tasty. I rather like the dainty tongue thing, darling V. One's eating practices, like most things, are overly subjugated to habit—here is a sunny wake-up, a bit of vinegar under the nose, our little lambkin's tongue, bleating away in Brazilian cocoa."

Throughout dinner, Vernon has been uncharacteristically silent. To have Kit here is beyond dreaming. With her health in ruin, she has spent whole days either inert or in some opposite, frenzied state, but Kit has finally arrived to nurse her, cure her of the Mary Robinson malady. As Matilda's chirping commentary and Eugene's dry accompaniments continue, Vernon, with quick glances, admires her friend.

"Thou, Clementina, hath a fresh perspective on Vernon's endless vagaries," says Matilda. "The thing thee may most enjoy, if thee are here that long, if thee indeed can bear us beyond a fortnight, are the out-of-doors theatricals Vernon puts on from time to time for the children of the *contadini*, the local peasants. Last year's was quite a production. I believe she did a Gozzi play, an adaptation. Carlo Gozzi, the Venetian playwright."

A ragged, stertorous blast of snoring, feigned or genuine, erupts from Eugene's prone form.

Giving her son a glance at once withering and affectionate, Matilda tosses down her napkin and rises, unperturbed. "Well then. While Eugene takes his postprandial nap, I shall be off to join Henry, who awaits me with a lantern in the garden. My errant husband and I take a stroll every evening before bed. Good digestion followed by perambulation—Henry's sole cure for every malady."

For the first time since she had arrived hours before, Kit—aside from Eugene, recumbent and genuinely snoring—is alone with Vernon. Thrusting her long, slim legs straight out in front of her, raising her arms overhead and stretching with luxuriant abandon, she springs up, strides to the fire, pokes at it until the flames leap high and cast sparks, then lopes across the room to kneel before Vernon. Draping her arms around her friend's neck, Kit leans in to kiss one cheek, then the other, followed, more lingeringly, by a kiss on her friend's lips.

"Divine feast, darling. Splendid. So . . . antique. Pigeons' feet, sheep's tongues, chocolate. Now, shall thee escort me up to my room, help me to settle in? What say thee, delectable Vernon?"

V.

———⟨∞⟩———

Two black bicycles, each with its woven rattan basket. Two sturdy ponies, black, with white splashes, named Mr. and Mrs. Horse. Two walking sticks carved smooth from the same oak branch. Two minds, clever and quick, two hearts . . . Deux. Due. Zwei. Two. Twin. Twinned. Entwined. One.

With my hand guiding Sylvia's, pressing pen to her page, I gaze back upon my life with Kit, those years when my reputation as a formidable mind was at its brightest, when my friend Mr. James—Henry—proclaimed I was the one British person in all of Florence worth holding a conversation with. But I was also what Italians call brutta. And too easily wounded to rage. At birth, my mother sacrificed me to Athena, virgin goddess of reason, so by the time I met Kit, my brain was weary, nerves tightly wound, heart a dumb organ.

Each day, Sylvia-from-the-forest comes nearer the truth. Has left her research, her books, for what I give her, moves far beyond moronic academic questions: 1) was I genuinely "queer?" 2) did I have a physical (sexual) relationship with Kit or any other woman? 3) was I as unattractive as has been *said? Scholars exploiting ambiguity to climb a step higher in their careers—writing tiresome books, dull papers, yesterday a Vernon Lee seminar in Paris, tomorrow a Vernon Lee conference in Rome or Budapest—who reads, who listens? Who listened when, old and deaf, I <u>demanded</u> no biography ever be written of me? "I absolutely prohibit any biography of me. My life is my own, and I leave that to nobody." My exact words, <u>quoted</u> in the two biographies published so far, others under way. Who listens?*

I am continuously disinterred, erroneously labeled. With the sole exception of my Adorable Listener, True Biographer, Boswellian Darling, unwashed, beautiful, living on scraps. She eats like a cat. Copies down the scenes I instill in her, depicts the images I cultivate in her. Precisely rendered, true.

How quickly she has stepped out of that old, sad persona, the betrayed wife. What does it matter whose clothing she wears, whether she speaks with anyone else, whether she bathes, eats, or sleeps? All seduction is supernatural. (Supernature, superior to nature.) With my brain lodged in hers, we become one stately residence.

A cat, I hunt my songbird. As Palma the shepherd, I protect my darling mistress. She senses this, and, brave soul, is only a little frightened.

Tonight she stands before the long glass, the same glass I, too, have stood naked before. Takes the measure of her body, its girl's womb intact. Touches her breasts, still beautiful, puts her hands to her face. Unpins her auburn hair, still abundant, beginning to gray, gazes into her own loneliness. Then sees it all. Sits naked at her desk, takes down, page after page, what I whisper to her to write. I am close enough to smell her bare skin, milky, half-sweet. Very soon now, within hours, I will scribe her solitary blankness, caress her rosy, concealed margins.

Sylvia

LAUNDRY. REWASHED BY RAIN, stiffened by sunlight, soiled by birds, pitted with rust from the metal hinges of clothespins, strewn on the floor, in need of cleaning again. Both desks littered with unwashed bowls, wineglasses, papers, photographs, books. Every morning when Sylvia wakes, they stare down at her, Hindu mystics, Christian saints. Ascetics. It must be their influence, she thinks, why she decides, this Sunday morning, to walk to church.

Coming downstairs, hair still uncombed, having slept in the clothes she had worn the day before—or was it the day before that?—Sylvia picks through whatever Remo has left out. Bowls of ruby-skinned cherries, ripe peaches, the day's vegetables—radishes, spinach. A round tin of English biscuits, a package of stale *grissini*. Offerings. Almost always at a distance, Remo. Part of the landscape, nature spirit. Lame, goat-legged Pan.

Holding the astronomer's little map, shakily sketched in blue ink, Sylvia climbs uphill, the sun hot overhead. She climbs past olive groves, shorn fields with neatly bound rolls of hay, finally reaching San Martino, a small fifteenth-century church. Less than twenty people are in attendance, three or four Italian families wearing dark blue or black, a few tourists in bright summer colors. Sylvia slips into a middle pew beside an elderly woman, elegantly dressed, her hair pinned in a wispy chignon. The Sunday Mass, an Albanian priest officiating, without flowers or music, is as unadorned as the church's gray stone interior. At the end of the Lord's Prayer, the woman extends her hand to wish Sylvia peace, *pace,* and later, in the stone courtyard, introduces herself as Countess Oriana Baldini. During their brief conversation, Sylvia learns that the countess knows Natalia, Giustina, the Alberini family, and has visited Villa il Palmerino a number of times, though lately, poor health has kept her at home. "The same few families, going back centuries, live here," she tells Sylvia. "We all know one another. I went to Natalia and Lorenzo's wedding years ago, at this church."

After saying good-bye to the countess, Sylvia consults her map and walks uphill past San Martino's monastery, eventually reaching Le Cave di Maiano, a locally famous restaurant concealed within rolling, wooded hills. Luciano Pavarotti had brought his family here; a fleet of black limousines moving at a snail's pace along the parched roads had once brought Jacqueline Kennedy here. A waiter leads Sylvia to a flagstone patio shaded by linden trees, brushes a few fallen leaves off of her table. It is still early; there is only one other guest, a very old man, formally dressed. Answering her inquiry, the waiter says this gentleman eats the same lunch at the same time every day at Le Cave. And yes, the single car she had seen in the parking lot, an ancient, perfectly preserved silver Mercedes, is his. The man is well known in Florence, very famous, but the waiter, protective of his guest's privacy, will divulge only his first name, Alberto. Eating with solemn pleasure, Alberto never once looks up from his plate, and the moment he is finished, stands up, and with the waiter's help, is led to his car. A young woman comes out from the restaurant with Sylvia's lunch—*crostini, gnocchi al pecorino, e bistecca alla fiorentina*. She eats slowly, savoring her food, as wonderful as Richard Asquith had promised it would be, sits awhile before paying her bill. She leaves just as Italian families, dressed for the church service they have just attended, talking gaily, arrive. As she walks downhill, past shorn, tawny fields, the olive trees with their black, dull-lustred fruits, a stream of expensive cars passes her, more families heading to Le Cave.

The next Sunday, Sylvia ventures out again, this time to the second place the astronomer had recommended, the music school. Unfortunately, Palma is following, loping along the busy, heavily trafficked road, oblivious to cars, to anything but Sylvia. Afraid the dog will be hit by a car, Sylvia yells, picks up a stone, aims. When the small rock strikes Palma's flank, the dog retreats, slinks back in the direction of home. Good. Being mean worked. Sylvia keeps walking. A minute or so later, she turns, sees Palma, scabby and yellow, lurking behind a shrub, watching her. Frustrated, Sylvia ducks behind a massive iron entrance gate, hoping Palma, by losing sight of her, will grow discouraged, head for home. Long minutes pass. The dog, inexhaustibly patient, waits for her to reappear. Sylvia strides back, speaks to Palma, reasons with her, explains she is going to a music concert, where dogs are not allowed. Ridiculous, but this sallow, coarse-bristled old dog seems to have an eerie, if obstinate, intelligence, so she actually hopes, desperately hopes, Palma will understand what she is saying. *Vai a casa,* she concludes in her sternest voice, then walks resolutely ahead. Palma follows. Sylvia gives up.

She enters the small concert space, pays for her ticket, is shown to her seat, begins reading her program. Chopin, played by Pietro De Maria, the first selection *Ballata n. 1 in sol minore, op. 23.* . . . All at once, the well-dressed Italians sitting in the row in front of her begin gesturing excitedly to one another. She follows the object of their attention. Palma, long, low, wild-looking, is inside the concert hall, skulking past the black Steinway.

"Bestiaccia maledetta!" an Italian woman says directly behind her. What a terrifying animal! Then a child begins to sob, as a young, well-dressed man who appears to be in charge of things, stands before the audience, shouting in Italian. "Whose dog is this? Whose dog, please?" he asks. Sylvia considers pretending she doesn't know whose dog it is, but Palma is bounding up the steps, heading straight toward her. She stands up, grabs hold of the dog's greasy old leather collar, and, apologizing profusely—*"Mi dispiace, mi dispiace"*—to everyone she steps over and passes, drags the dog outside. After giving Palma a stern lecture and ordering her to sit, which Palma, astonishingly, does, Sylvia slips back inside, sinks into a vacant chair near the door at the exact moment the pianist steps onstage, bows, sits. It is stirring, deeply emotional, the opening Chopin

ballad, but Sylvia cannot concentrate, hears only disjointed
bits. For five minutes or so, as Palma sits next to the glass
entry doors, staring mournfully, silently, in at her, Sylvia's
hopes rise. But when Palma begins scratching at the glass
door, whining piteously, she leaves.

Infuriated, embarrassed, she doesn't look at the dog or
speak to it on the walk home. Doesn't care if it gets hit, dies.
It doesn't, of course. Palma is nothing if not devoted to staying close to Sylvia. Once they are inside the villa's property,
she forgives Palma, pets her, realizing it is not so much she,
Sylvia, looking out for the dog, but that, for whatever reason, Palma seems determined to watch over her.

Bernard Berenson

Villa il Palmerino
San Gervasio
June 1889

The afternoon is uncommonly hot as the Harvard graduate, ruthless in his ambitions, trudges up the shaded road.
Important others have made this necessary pilgrimage,
and tucked into his front pocket is a letter of introduction
from one of them. Young Bernard Berenson has read and
reviewed several of Vernon Lee's books in *The Harvard
Monthly,* and now he is on a secular mission to meet her.
Climbing steadily uphill, Berenson, a slight-figured connoisseur of Renaissance art, generally regarded as articu-
late and poisonously witty, imagines himself meeting the
famous Vernon Lee, charming her with his pedigree, his
precocity, his enviable elegance. In reality, he is thirsty,
peevish, tired of walking, and this appears to have become
a pilgrimage in the most tedious religious sense. His left
boot chafes against his heel as he wonders where it will
end, this infernal road, this rural trot. Famished as well,

he begins to hope she will invite him to stay for dinner. He has heard the rumors of course, of her abrasiveness, a suffer-no-fools kind of thing, of her ugliness, a sort of third-sexed creature, but still . . . so brilliant an intellect, spontaneous, reckless, impulsive—it has been said she spits ink—and so well connected in the tight-knit society of Italian artists and critics. Well, he will act no fool, and he sees no reason not to expect that mutual affection, or at least an affectation of mutual affection, should be the outcome of this first meeting.

At last he comes upon the gaudy yellow villa, set like a discarded trunk alongside the road. When he knocks, gripping a brass pharaoh's head centered on the dark green door, a shabbily dressed manservant answers, leads him down a short graveled path through a neglected, messy garden to the villa itself, up two flights of stone stairs to a pair of ivory-colored double doors. The servant draws open both doors as Berenson removes his hat, smoothes back his hair, limps his way toward the Presence. What a retinal impression! He will recall this, years later, in his private diaries. A woman neither old nor young, dressed as a man, slumped in a Windsor chair before an unlit hearth, surrounded—no, engulfed—by a chittering group of equally mannish hens. Eager to secure his place in the elite art world of Florence, young Bernard Berenson has stumbled upon one of Vernon Lee's famous *cultes*. It is well known, her mesmerizing effect upon certain sorts of young women. One of these devotees—Amy Levy, a very minor British poet—had recently committed suicide, breathing coal smoke, because of Vernon. Sitting closest, neatly folded up at Vernon's feet like a

fan, is her Scottish lover, Clementina Anstruther-Thomson.
Outfitted like a man as well, a sketchbook splayed on her lap,
Anstruther-Thomson, who is at least handsome, records
the proceedings, catching *les mots précieux* as they fall from
Vernon Lee's pale, pendulous horse lips. At his unexpected,
uninvited entrance, the room's excited, high-pitched buzz
of female voices dies away, as if submerged by a dark, heavy
wave, and he finds himself withering beneath a collectively
cold and haughty gaze, a gaze that interrogates, demands to
know, Who is he?

The ensuing visit, an exercise in humiliation for young
Berenson, bears no resemblance to the social triumph he
had envisioned. There is no dinner, either, not so much as
a cool tumbler *d'eau*. Individual persons make way for him,
grudgingly, as he approaches the Presence, drawing forth
from his pocket a much-creased letter of introduction,
a letter from a person of such insignificance in Florence,
a female person so far removed from importance, such a
peripheral member of the Anglo-American community as
to be a mere string of shawl fringe, yet it is all he has—this
letter, which, as it turns out, will be more of an insult to
Vernon Lee than no letter at all.

Wordlessly, she seizes the letter, opens it, scans its contents in less than seconds before fixing him with that bright,
greedy green gaze of hers. People, he sees at once, are no
better than books to her, ideas to be stolen, repositories of
whatever she can glean to feed her rapacious bird-of-prey
mind. Well, he thinks, this male repository, this vertical
body of ideas, will hold his tongue, bide his time.

Silence swells, hangs in the room while she steadily regards him. Blood rushes to the roots of his hair; the dust on his boots turns to mud, the uneasiness in his stomach to noxious gas. He is being scolded, made aware that he has *trespassed*.

When at last she does speak, Vernon Lee's voice is imperious, nasal, high-pitched. "You must tell us what you saw, Mr. Berenson—no, tell us what you *felt* when you first stood before Titian's painting *Sacred and Profane Love*. You've seen it, haven't you, since you are just come from Rome? You know the imbecilic title is a false one, bestowed by some moralizing, scandalized idiot? Titian had no such dichotomy in mind. The painting was a commission, intended to celebrate the marriage of the fifteenth-century Venetian Niccolò Aurelio to the young widow Laura Bagarotto. Choose another painting if you prefer. Another subject. We simply wish to hear you speak. Prior to your remarkable entrance, we were discussing the Titian—but you may select something entirely new. The point is to introduce yourself. Show us something of your mind."

A trap. The only thing is to be bold, dodge the trap she has maliciously set for him. Do something to stupefy this roomful of whinging Sapphites. Something to enthrall, to conquer without once having to stoop. Berenson, intent on becoming a man of significance, is nothing if not canny.

Bowing deeply from the waist, first to Her Holy Terror, then to her long-nosed lover, then in a sweeping, generalized way to the entire gathering of chits, harpies—not a sweet bloom among them—he ingratiates himself.

"I should not deign to offer any knowledge superior to that of Ms. Lee, but of late, I have been poring over certain ancient shards of Arabic poetry. With your indulgence, I will recite pieces I have recently memorized, afterward revealing some of their authors' history. By proceeding down this narrow tributary of Oriental elucidation so as to . . ."

In less than an hour, young Bernard Berenson, Harvard graduate, is gimping down the selfsame road he had pilgrimed his way up, unfed, unwatered, unnerved. His reception had been rude in the extreme, although Anstruther-Thomson, cast in the role of the favored, most senior sycophant, had not unkindly escorted him to the villa's gate, saying "We would very much like to have you return and visit us again, Mr. Berenson, without today's distraction." She had then tossed him the name of an influential Italian critic, Carlo Placci, to whom he should feel welcome to introduce himself, at the recommendation of Vernon Lee, a name he nipped deftly from the ground, a scrap of meat to carry off and sniff at later.

Thus, he is not altogether displeased. His Arabian poetry had saved him; he hadn't made a stupendous (*passez-moi le mot!*) ass of himself; he had secured an invitation to return to il Palmerino and been awarded a fairly important name tendered with Vernon Lee's costive blessing. Carlo Placci's would be the first door to swing open for him, with her, Frightful Brain, turning the knob. The enterprise had hardly gone as he had imagined, though it was consistently true of Bernard that his imaginings inclined toward the grandiose. For the moment, *quand même*, he is content. He has come away, at least, with gains.

Villa il Palmerino
San Gervasio
January 1892

For complicated reasons, it will be nearly three years before
he finds himself once again at Villa il Palmerino. This time,
it will be winter and a sneezing Anstruther-Thomson, bun-
dled in a black cape and mitered cap, who meets him at the
gate after he pounds the icy pharaoh's head against the dark
green door. She escorts him into the same upstairs salon,
orders tea be brought up, pokes at the fire. Later, when they
are in the midst of an awkward, faltering conversation,
something incomprehensible about art, physiology, and the
poor of London's East End, Vernon bangs in, a small gust
of a person, barely five feet, in full, ridiculous-looking riding costume, crop in hand, tossing her riding helmet upon
a yellow brocade chair with so poor an aim, it misses the
chair and tumbles to the floor. There are no other visitors
that afternoon; he is alone with two half women, scorch-
ing before a fire pungent with bundles of dried lavender,
and the conversation soon prickles, flares into argument.
Whatever he ventures to say, Vernon objects to or finds
disagreement with—shouting him down at several points,
while Anstruther-Thomson, well-bred animal, sleek and
removed, merely turns her gaze upon him with solemn
astonishment whenever he challenges Vernon, dares to dis-
agree. Vernon, energized by combat, yields no intellectual
ground. He begins to see that to triumph, he must court
her, try his hardest to be outwardly deferential, appear to

acquiesce. Still, she is all MOUTH, this woman he has privately taken to calling La Vernonia. Such bellowings from that loose, red maw, an artillery of facts, theories, quotations. How she opines! Outrageously informed, unstoppable. Really, he can't stand her, and he definitely cannot ameliorate her bad opinion of him. A woman with a passionate nature who has *"never had a man's love,"* he will write to an acquaintance ... therein lies the entire trouble with Vernon Lee.

During this visit, a third, weird, purgatorial thing lurks in one corner of the room, gothic, backlit by flames from the fire—a half brother, served up on a wheeled bier, an eternally expiring poet and piece of furniture—Eugene Lee-Hamilton. A ghoulish tableau, just as William James had described it, morbid and ghastly. Berenson will be treated to an entire afternoon of this "viewing," as of a corpse, of Eugene. La Vernonia in her riding couture, scarlet-cheeked, fresh in from a solitary gallop, and Anstruther-Thomson, suffering a beastly head cold that leaves her snuffling and rheumy-eyed, her aristocratic nose red and raw and weeping ... and Le Cadavre, rotating its head from time to time toward Bernard, who half-dreads a worm will creep out from one of its eyes—a most troglodytic scene. He can scarcely wait to write about it.

"You will come with us to the galleries tomorrow, Mr. Berenson? The Uffizi, principally. We would be pleased for you to observe one of our kinetic experiments, Kit's, rather—measuring her physiologic response to a set of sculptures. Her aesthetic empathy. It is all part of the research we have undertaken for an article we believe will be accorded singular attention once it is published."

Catastrophe, Berenson thinks, standing up to take his leave, declining the dinner invitation, particularly after Le Cadavre wrathfully pronounces the cook's fare inedible. What a brash, rude, brilliant, savagely invigorating, infuriating afternoon. Berenson's forehead aches from it. Vernon, naturally, did all the talking—with the others, aside from his own occasional contribution (argument), silent as chinoiserie urns.

Theirs will be a long, turbulent, semivindictive association. In correspondence, Bernard Berenson refers to Vernon Lee as "the Palmerino," "the Palmerino Sibyl," "La Vernonia," and less often, "the Hierophant." A witty gossip and tireless social climber, he ridicules her behind her back, while in her presence he takes pains to be obsequious, his tongue knowing just how much oil to use to smooth his speech. After each visit, he rushes off to record his spiteful impressions, his waspish opinion of the Sibyl.

Upon the first of their several excursions together to the Uffizi galleries, he attends a demonstration of La Vernonia's latest theories on art and human physiognomy. Observes Anstruther-Thomson enact several of her bewildering depictions of bodily sensation before an unimpressive group of Roman funerary statues, concluding with a bizarre solo pantomime before Caravaggio's *Medusa.*

Although it warps every fiber in his mind, Bernard Berenson maintains an amiable outward relation with Vernon Lee. He knows he will always be a callow youth in her eyes, and, as such, forced to endure her savage critiques of his mind (he is no critic, she never tires of telling him, but that other, lesser thing—a connoisseur). Unsparing critic herself, she dips every one of his written sentences in an acid of faintest praise.

Her intimacies, her suspect intimacies with women, continue to repulse him, particularly the long-term affair with Anstruther-Thomson, who trots eternally at Vernon's heels, a lively, docile hound. Still, La Vernonia does, at times, enchant him, and during those times, he comes close to regarding her as a friend. On one of his infrequent treks up to Villa il Palmerino, he finds no one at home. Sauntering back down the hill, he encounters her driving, of all things, a pony cart, with Anstruther-Thomson and a visiting sculptress from Berlin, stout, lively, and smoking a cigar, squeezed between them. The cart is heaped with wildflowers and herbs gathered from the woods, and perhaps because Vernon has for once pulled her nose out of a book and stuck it instead into the fragrant delights of nature, she is friendly, and stops the cart to greet him. And as Berenson stands in the dirt road, hat removed in deference to the three half women, Vernon retrieves a small red leather book from somewhere inside of her loose shirt and brusquely hands it over to him, telling him he may borrow it until she gets him his own copy. It is a book about the sixteenth-century Venetian painter Lorenzo Lotto's frescoes in the Oratorio Suardi in Trescore.

Delighted by the coincidence, he hands up several rare photos of portraits by Lotto he has brought to show her. She studies them a long while, thanks him, returns them. As he walks back down into the city, Bernard admits to himself that her intelligence had been much more digestible, less pontifical, less hierophantic (which is the moment he conceived of this new moniker for her, the Hierophant, though since hardly anybody knows its meaning, he will use it less and less before dropping it altogether). Perhaps he should suggest that, in future, they meet out-of-doors, like shepherds. Perhaps they will prefer one another more *en plein air*.

But they will never prefer one another. There will be a scandal, an accusation of plagiarism by Berenson that will boil on until after Kit's death, when Vernon will suddenly dismiss the quarrel as a mere *boutade*, a whim, and warily befriend Berenson, now her neighbor. In her final years, a thoroughly deaf Vernon, accompanied by a large brass ear trumpet hanging from her neck by a black silk cord, will be a frequent, even welcome, visitor to Villa I Tatti. Her luncheon conversations with Berenson will be marked by one chief eccentricity: Whenever she speaks, she places the trumpet to her ear; whenever he responds, speaking so rapidly that he makes the exact sound, as Vernon puts it, of a hen laboring at an egg, she withdraws it.

A Chair, a Wall, a Jar

The chair is a bilateral object, so the two eyes are equally active. They meet the two legs of the chair at the ground and run up both sides simultaneously. There is a feeling as if the width of the chair were pulling the two eyes wide apart during the process of following the upward line of the chair. Arrived at the top the eyes are no longer pulled apart; on the contrary, they converge inward along the top of the chair . . .
— *"Beauty and Ugliness," C.A.T.*
(Clementina Anstruther-Thomson)

Travel with deep purpose, Vernon writes in her Commonplace Book, is preferable to the shallows of sightseeing. One has only to observe all the poor, disgruntled things stranded in outdoor cafés in Florence, nursing tired feet, lamenting aching necks and diminishing wallets, to realize how enervating it is to gaze upon sites and objects elevated by the opinions of others, chiefly Baedeker in his tiresome guidebooks. *"For those with a mutual project, such as Kit's and mine, with its key question: What causes a work of art to be perceived as beautiful or ugly?—travel is exhilarating. We are resolved to answer a certain aesthetic question with a system, a map of prescribed visits to galleries, churches and museums. (Note to self: list places!) In these select spots, we choose our objects of study. . . ."*

For each "experiment," Kit Anstruther-Thomson enters an altered consciousness before conveying every sensation her body is experiencing. As her self-appointed amanuensis, Vernon records Kit's barely audible words with a rushed scratching, her pen clawing across the page, leaving black trails of ink.

The earliest experiments are conducted at Villa il Palmerino. They begin with Vernon's writing chair, followed by a blank wall, which proves not to be blank, and conclude with an empty jar of thick green glass used to store oil from Palmerino's olive trees. All three objects—chair, wall, jar—persuade them of the merit of their inquiry, and beyond merit, they dare to believe they have stumbled upon a key to the universe. Kit and Vernon next draw up an itinerary of travel, noting sites and objects of art they most wish to visit. In studying the impact of each of these objets d'art upon Kit's physiognomy—heart rate, respiration, and muscular tension—they intend to prove a subtle connection between works of art and the human body. Similar theories have been put forth by William James and others, but a detailed examination of the human body's visceral response to objects is the first of its kind, a landmark experiment.

Sartorial focus, caution in dress, they agree, is an aid to scientific objectivity. For the first experiment, with Vernon's writing chair the object to be studied, Kit chooses a linen smock and loose pants. She wears no shoes, goes unshod, discalced, as Vernon calls it, so the soles of her feet are open and unencumbered. Her hair is unpinned and loose; she wears no jewelry. She must be as close to pure animal form as possible. Complete nudity is the ideal, but how, Kit reasons, could she possibly gad about naked in private, much less in public museums and galleries, without social and legal consequence? Loose clothing is an acceptable compromise. For her part, Vernon wears a black suit of Italian merino wool. The severe cut and color turn her shapeless and fearless, accentuate her long, heavy jaw, parchment skin, and chopped graying hair. Rising from such negative ground is Vernon's newest habit of chewing and rolling her pendulous lower lip around as though it were separate from the rest of her face, a nervous habit Kit says she has seen horses acquire, although never a person.

For the second experiment, the wall Vernon selects is on the second floor of Casa Paget, part of the common room used, on occasion, for chamber concerts and dinner parties. On the morning of the wall experiment, Kit and Vernon lounge in silk morning wrappers and wool slippers. Disheveled, unbound, they sip strong black coffee. Vernon smokes. It is the second experiment in as many days, and already they have forgotten their costumes.

Vernon neatly inks the date and hour into her notebook, writes down a brief but objective description of the wall and its location. Seated at the head of the dining table, pen poised, she stares at Kit, who now poses before the wall barefoot, legs spread wide, arms loose at her sides, palms opened outward to receive the subtlest of sensations. Shutting her eyes tight to SEE more precisely, Kit begins to whisper as Vernon scribbles her words: ". . . the wall a solid white substance, my lungs pull apart as my eyes travel up the wall, as I exhale they scan from the right to left corner, then left to right corner, my pulse accelerates as I near the wall's center. Now here is something most strange, breath quickening, muscles achieving a kind of alertness, and something else—I am FEELING—is in these walls, beneath the surface blankness, the plainness, I sense, feel—imagery! . . . color! . . . it is a <u>scene</u>, very old, whitewashed over."

Though it never happens again, on this particular morning, Kit discovers a miraculous ability of the body and mind in tandem: the gift of sensing, feeling, that which is invisible to the human eye. Something lies beneath the white surface of the wall; she is certain of it.

Vernon summons three art preservationists to examine the wall. With meticulous care, they uncover a large fifteenth-century fresco, Crusader knights on horseback, bearing palm fronds, returning presumably from the Holy Lands. Painted perhaps for the original family who lived here, the revealed fresco is badly chipped in places and faded to palest ocher, indigo, gold. Vernon confesses she has always *felt something* whenever she walked past that particular wall—the fresco, pressing up from its whitewashed place of concealment!

The third and last experiment at the villa, the empty green jar, yields nothing of interest. The chair had been useful. But the wall fresco! By the time Bernard Berenson joins them at the Uffizi as an invited observer, Vernon and

Kit's experimentations have come dangerously close, as one critic will point out, to theatrical absurdity.

Berenson stands at a deliberate remove from the others, face pinched into an expression of fastidious distaste. He is in a gallery of the Uffizi, along with several fashionably dressed devotees of Vernon's *culte,* watching as Kit, barefoot, wearing outlandish bloomers and a peasant tunic, writhes on the floor in front of a dull Greek sculpture before bursting out, *"Look! It sings!"* Vernon, shoving her lower lip out and chewing on it, gazes rapturously at Kit, causing Berenson to later remark in his journal that La Vernonia hunts beauty like Sibyl in pursuit of Aphrodite. Making matters worse, she continues to look down on him with disdain, even if he is the taller of the two. Continues to exclude him, bar him from crucial introductions to persons of importance. Her referencing him as a "connoisseur of the Renaissance"—connoisscurship being a new and questionable field of study—is an ongoing insult. No matter how his star rises, her actions imply that she will never take him seriously. So when "Beauty and Ugliness," by Vernon Lee and Kit Anstruther-Thomson, appears in the *Contemporary Review*, the vindictive feud that arises from its publication is no surprise to anyone.

Astonished by Berenson's florid letter of accusation, Vernon conceals it from Kit, who is in a state of brain exhaustion. But her protective resolve weakens one evening during dinner, when Kit presses her as to her black mood. Vernon answers by fetching the vile letter, reading it aloud, and denouncing it as a petty bit of epistolary arsenic couched in artificial phrases. Plagiary is lethal accusation, and Berenson, an egotistic, ill-tempered ass, insinuates they have stolen not only his ideas, his obiter dicta, but, in certain cases, copied his very phrases into their "misguided" essay. Surprise ambush from a pygmy spirit! Never averse to argument, Vernon is eager to fire back. But Kit, already mentally strained, weeps. In Clementina Anstruther-Thomson's aristocratic, insular mind-set of horses, hounds, and foxhunts, dishonor is fatal. To be accused of theft like this is tantamount to an honorable gentleman being falsely accused of cheating at cards. Vernon, she weeps on, may be invigorated by such scandal, but for her, such an unexpungeable stain will destroy her.

Not bothering to disguise her fury or soften her disgust at his outrageous accusation, Vernon writes to Berenson the next day. Years later, soon after Kit's death and at his own wife Mary's urging, Bernard Berenson will insist he never meant any harm, that his *jesting*, admittedly in poor taste, had been misinterpreted. For her part, Vernon will say she overreacted. Until then, their feud will rage off and on for nearly twenty years.

But the immediate upshot of the scandal is its deleterious effect upon Kit. The insult is grave, her nature too innocent, too naive. She had tried throughout the experiments and writing of the article to keep up with Vernon's intellect and mental stamina, but at the price of her own nerves. Now she is disgraced. A distant cousin of Kit's, who had known her since childhood, had early on warned Vernon that Kit could never stand up to the strenuous mental tasks Vernon kept setting her. "She is an equestrienne," the cousin wrote. "Clementina is an athlete, high-spirited, and curious, an artist of very minor talent who, as you know, once dabbled at the Slade under the tutelage of John Sargent's master teacher, Carolus-Duran. But she is no scholar; her mind is fickle, scattered. She won't bear up." But Vernon had waved off the warning; now Kit's brain is indeed broken. In the autumn and early winter months, as "Beauty and Ugliness" receives a trickle of faint, damning praise, along with an occasional scathing criticism for its weak hypotheses, Kit retreats. Takes to designing puppet theaters, reading fairy tales and fables, taking long walks or riding her horse. She wants no company, refuses to think, is unable to think, discuss art or aesthetics, much less respond to negative reviews. She recedes, turns child-like, shuts Vernon out. This wall of politeness lasts weeks, until one evening Kit walks into Vernon's study holding a letter, a set expression on her flawless face. Vernon is strangely unperturbed by her flat announcement that she has decided to leave for London within the week to nurse a friend, Mrs. Sylvia Head, a Catholic, who suffers from some unknown ailment she hopes Kit can soothe and perhaps even cure.

Neither Kit nor Vernon mention the real cause of their separation, the Berenson scandal. There is no quarrel, no recrimination. Kit simply declares, in that straightforward way of hers, that she is needed elsewhere. The amputation is bloodless, quick enough to keep Vernon from feeling much of anything until after Kit is gone, when her absence suddenly becomes an enlarging wound, a sepsis, darkening and staining everything.

V.

For all of my loquaciousness—Virginia Woolf once said "listening to Vernon Lee talk is like listening to a big, garrulous baby"—I could not control my own biology. Had no say over my own nature. My conversations were aggressive, my monologues meant to conquer society. With my "io mi domando" twenty times a day—charging into every room with debate, argument, memorization, and question—I dominated. Ruled!

Or so I thought. With the twin defects of a perfect mind and an imperfect heart, I seized upon a ploy to anchor Kit to my side. Together, I told her, we will ask Art's central question. Together we will travel and locate Beauty's power.

In the end, I drove Beauty away. She fled to save herself.

If Mary Robinson's loveliness appealed universally, Kit's was the beauty of an epicene—androgynous, superbly limbed, that superior beauty of animals who are proud, yet lack all vanity. I gazed for jealous hours first upon Mary, then Kit, in some futile hope of lightening my own features.

I see it now, of course. In the afterlife, one understands things differently. My "villainy" lay in simple jealousy, in my hunger to devour the minds of others. A king's mistake, and like most kings, from sovereignty came isolation.

There is something much harder for me to speak about. Following the shame of Mary's rejection, I suffered paralysis. Not like Eugene's, but all at once I loathed touch. An embrace horrified me. A kiss made me ill.

And though she had rarely reproached me for it, Kit left me that first time not because of Berenson and his false accusation of plagiary, which did, of course, wound her, but because I would not let her touch me. I refused to let her kiss me or see me unclothed. After Mary, all I wanted was that naked, dangerous part of myself—my heart, most of all—dead.

Eventually, missing her, I made my way to London. Found Kit at Mrs. Head's, yet another chronic invalid invoking the tyranny of illness. My Divine Nurse could never resist a weaker woman's need of her, and because of my brother, I knew the power of illness, how it sinks sickly talons into those who are strong and well. Finding Kit in thrall to an invalid, I returned home dejected, wondering how I could ever persuade her to return to our former happy life at Palmerino.

After a chance remark by a friend, I hit upon a way to recover Kit's affections: a children's theatrical. I wrote to her:

Come back to Palmerino for the month of June. We will put on an out-of-doors play for the children of the peasant families here in San Gervasio and Maiano. I am nearly settled on Gozzi's <u>L'Augellino Belverde</u>, a magical bit of eighteenth-century Venetian commedia dell'arte. I've enclosed a copy for you, chérie, you'll see that it fairly sparkles with fantasy and real wit. A king and his evil mother, a set of twins with *their mother buried alive in the sewer of the king's castle, a mysterious green bird with magic powers, a fountain of singing apples . . . do say you will come! And June, Giugno, as you remember, is the most divine portion of year at Palmerino. And your divine white rose, the cutting you sent years ago from Charleton House, will be in full snowy bloom. We shall dine every evening out of doors, enchanted by its faintly obscene fragrance. Others will join us, Eugene, of course, and I've already engaged two lovely young Italian girls as well as the Pasolinis, the Cecchis, others who adore you. Oh, bon Coeur, do make your way to us at the beginning of June, and we shall have an unforgettable month.*

Say yes, my dear! Your room awaits you, unchanged.

V

—postscript: bring Mrs. H. if you wish,
or at least reassure her of your return.

One thing more:

Kit was Eugene's Christ. Because of her, my brother—that half Lazarus—rose up from his bier. When both Dr. Erbes and the famed Paris neurologist, Dr. Charcot, could recommend nothing more for him, it was Kit who persuaded him—by her own vitality—by energy and optimism—that he must get up, walk, live. The miracle happened three days after Mother died, which I am convinced had a great deal to do with it. Mother had always coddled Eugene, preferred him paralyzed, so he might never abandon her. After all, she judged Father worthless. All men were worthless except Eugene, and of him she made a living relic. But once Matilda left us, breathing her last in Kit's arms (Kit nursing her with a steadfastness I did not possess, too fearful of succumbing to my own abyss), once Mother had been laid to rest in the Allori Cemetery, that drab little acreage of English decomposition, Eugene discovered strength in his limbs. With Kit propping him up, helping him stagger from one room to another, then eventually out-of-doors, he was on his feet and off. Within months, he had climbed Mount Vesuvius, sailed to America, sailed back, married, and fathered a child. All after the age of fifty, all after Mother's death!

Kit was Christ to all of us Pagets, until she fled, under the excuse of the Berenson scandal, to another woman, one who had not burdened and broken her by cold, corrosive inquiry into the influence of Art upon the Body.

Although Kit succeeded in nursing both my parents into their graves (Angel of Death) and in putting Eugene back on his feet (Angel of Life), still she had been unable to rouse me from my erotic paralysis.

Not until I lost Kit to London, to sickly Mrs. Head, did I suddenly, desperately, need to be awakened by her, to be touched, to yield.

Sylvia

⸺⊙⊙⊙⸺

IN HER ROOM, SHE SPENDS the remainder of the day leafing through all of the black-and-white photos she had ordered reproduced from library archives in Maine, where much of the material about Vernon Lee's life is stored. Photographs of Vernon, of her brother, Eugene, both before and during the time of his paralysis. Photos of Vernon's friends. Two of Kit, several of Mary. Photos taken while traveling, photos of Palmerino, one of two house servants, a white German shepherd posed between them. Sylvia turns that photograph over, studies the penciled handwriting, faint against the dark gray cardboard. *Fortunata and Beppe, with Neve.* Turns the photograph back over. Unless she's gone mad, Beppe is Remo's uncanny double. And Neve is Palma's.

She contemplates the photographs again, slowly this time and with a new thought. A thought so strange and unnerving, she puts them down, turns to something mundane and explicable: her e-mail.

Another e-mail from Philip—she ignores it like the others he has been sending her. She does read a new e-mail from Natalia, saying she has just returned from her dance project in Budapest and plans to host an informal dinner tomorrow evening for a few Italian friends, all writers and artists. It would be wonderful if Sylvia could join them. The dinner will be held outdoors at eight o'clock, on the loggia beneath Sylvia's window.

How timely. Natalia's invitation arrives just as she is questioning herself, worried that her concentration on Vernon Lee has become an obsession, and cannot obsession lead to madness? For instance, the astronomer, Richard Asquith, is he mad or simply a genius, living beyond the realm and scope of most people's minds? In the midst of her perilous speculation on madness, she receives an invitation to dine with living, presumably sane people, implying that she, Sylvia, is sane and alive, as well. The thought calms her. In fact, it gives her just the energy she needs to write down the next turn of events in Vernon's affair with Kit.

The concealed garden within the known garden. The play within the play. The kiss that will change, or seem to change, everything.

L'Augellino Belverde:
Dress Rehearsal

Villa il Palmerino
San Gervasio
June 1892

Eugene, a trussed pheasant on his platter, gazes, lugubri-
ous, at the ceiling. For days now, *no one* (that would mean
Violet) has bothered to read aloud to him or inquire about
the latest poem hotly fermenting in his head. He may as
well be a moldering broom straw orphaned from its broom,
a vacant birdcage befouled with sickly air, for all the notice
anyone (that would mean Violet) pays him. Even his idiot
valet has been conscripted, ordered into town to fetch
something or other. And that long horse of a girl, Kit, with
her high-pitched whinny and Violet, his hell-bound sister,
are all a-twitter on the other side of the room, chattering on
about their theatrical for the local peasant children (con-
descending notion!), plotting how to construct a stupid
water fountain, a tree with singing apples. Singing turds!

Gozzi's *L'Augellino Belverde, fiaba, fiaba, fiaba, fiabe, fiabe, fiabe,* stuffs their heads morning till night; they brook no other thought, talk of nothing but Gozzi, fairy tales and fables, horseshit. Eighteenth-century buffoonery, masks, singing fountains, preposterous events, a flapping green bird. *La commedia fiabesca*—fairy comedy, sheer uselessness. Bloody blazes! Even if no one listens, even if no one cares, Eugene feels compelled to speak his mind, speak it to himself at least. *I suppose your various gangrenous friends, Bags, will descend upon us like clacking locusts. You can be sure Maman is already tired, imagining them here, and Papa will vanish deep into the woods and shoot something. And those tiny rustic brats, here again! They'll be tearing through the gardens, uprooting and muddying things, trumpeting and vaulting over the hedges, baiting the dog—eating everything in sight. Like last year, unbearable.*

As if she overhears his self-pitying, scathing thoughts, Vernon gets up from the floor, where she and Kit have been painting a piece of stage scenery, and crosses the salon to stand over the prone and livid figure of her brother, acting the part of Lazarus of Bethany, unconvincingly this time. Due to Kit's Christ-like powers, for nearly a week, Eugene has begun to sit up; last night, he'd even stood, trembling, for a few dynamic seconds.

"Eugene. You are not paralyzed, merely jealous. I forbid you to spoil our fun, lest I recast you not as Calmon, the man-statue, a part you play to perfection, but as Tartagliona, the old queen, who gets reduced to a very nasty turtle by the play's end." She bends down, skims a fastidious kiss across Eugene's smooth, sallow cheek, scented with vetiver from his morning's shave. "When Kit and I are finished, I promise to sit beside you and hear your latest poem. My attention shall be yours alone, *mon frère.*"

Still sulking, Eugene refuses to speak until his sister relents and agrees to listen, immediately, to his recitation of "Sonnet Gold," his new creation.

> "*—or from old missals, where the gold defies*
> *Time's hand, in saints' bright aureoles and keeps,*
> *In angels' long straight trumpets, all is flash;*
>
> "*But chiefly from the crucible, where lies*
> *The alchemist's pure dream-gold.—While he sleeps,*
> *The poet steals it, leaving him the ash.*"

As he stops to dabble and fret over the phrase "pure dream-gold" (should it be "pure gold dream"?), Vernon sighs, pokes a few sugared violets in her brother's bushy white beard, straightens the laurel wreath gone lopsided on his head. As she hoped, he had come around, agreed to a minor role in Gozzi's play, the part of Calmon, moralizing man-statue (irony intended). Adept at memorization, he has solidly gotten his few lines.

When he finally settles on "pure dream-gold," Vernon stands, applauds. "Brilliant, brilliant, bravo! Violette hath crowned your poet's head with laurel, your bard's beard with sugared violets. And now, apologies, dear Eugene, Kit seems to have left us and escaped into the garden. I must go see what she is up to."

Mollified by his sister's brief attentions, Eugene feels a degree better, thinks he might try sitting, even standing once more. He'd like to briefly experience, however dizzyingly, the vertical world.

Costumed in a gold brocade frock coat, green silk waistcoat, lace cravat, gold breeches, high black boots, and a peruke, badly powdered, on her head, Vernon leans perilously far out of the upstairs salon window. She is watching Kit test her fountain of singing apples while simultaneously instructing three hired workers where to place the musicians' chairs and music stands—beneath, no, not so far beneath—the weeping willow tree. As Pulcinella, a stock character in commedia dell'arte, Kit is wearing a baggy white shirt, droopy white drawstring pants, and, on her head, a tall white *coppolone*, or "sugar loaf" hat. A bird's mask of stiffened black cloth dangles from a black ribbon down her back, its inky beak curving murderously upward.

Spotting Count Gozzi (Vernon) waving from the salon window upstairs, Pulcinella, philosopher of melancholy, breaks character, sweeps in the whole garden with a grand gesture. "Tomorrow's performance will be triumphant, dear Gozzi! I have sent Matilda into the kitchen to supervise the honey and aniseed cakes and asked your father to patrol the grounds for stray wildlife. Is Eugene on his way down or is he still playing the wrong part, pretending to be paralyzed? Tell him I need his help with a dozen or more things. Perhaps he will begin to walk, if only to please me."

The honey and aniseed cakes are another of Vernon's unearthed eighteenth-century recipes, plain but sweet enough, she hopes, to please the children. She stands for another moment at the scarlet-draped window, looking down into the small formal garden, listening to Kit explain something to the workers she'd initially hired to dig up the center of the lawn and found so useful, she'd kept them on. Kit has spent the past four weeks obsessed with designing and building her *fontana*. Even now, dozens of pen and ink sketches, accompanied by voluminous notes, are strewn around the dining area, and countless books on gardens and garden statuary have been left open, piled atop one another. She has spent hours sitting backward on a chair, barefoot, long legs tucked back, wearing only jodhpurs and a loose handmade tunic, paging through fountain designs, scribbling down directions on construction and materials. After drawing pages and pages of possibilities, some simple, others grandiose, she'd finally settled on a circular three-tiered *fontana* of white marble, a "magic" fountain designed to send water spraying upward with such force as to cause a dozen "apples," custom-ordered spheres of green glass from Murano, to "sing." Along with the three hired workers, Kit's magic *fontana* has cost Vernon a fortune.

But she has not dared refuse any expense proposed by Kit, has stifled any objection to cost or practicality. Nothing must stand in the way of Kit's enthusiasm. If she entices Kit with the possibility of endless theatricals and puppet shows for the children of the poor, Vernon is confident she will stay. For that joy, she is willing to compromise her scholar's life, to marry art with social cause under one roof, hers. Just as she thinks this, Pulcinella twirls ludicrously, loopily, blowing a courtly kiss up to Gozzi before lewdly sticking out her tongue. The workers turn away, embarrassed.

Vernon has reason to hope Kit might move back in with her. Her current life in London, volunteering with Girl Guides, nursing Mrs. Head, all this selfless service, tireless penitence, scourging of self, has aged Kit, made her look worn, seem less bright.

Then there is Vernon's secret, her more desperate need. Just that morning, she had slipped a cryptic note under Kit's bedroom door. *Past forty. Still unloved.*

The outdoor dining table is awash in dirty plates, half-empty serving bowls, half-filled goblets, discarded napkins, bottles of wine, pitchers of water, silver candelabra with amber candles lit, guttering low. Flies crawl everywhere. With her gold frock coat unbuttoned, lace cravat and waistcoat stained with dinner and wine, Gozzi bats at one persistent fly, while holding forth to her friends, crowded in under the pergola. Above them, the soft, crumpled faces of white roses give off a seductive, decaying scent. The dress rehearsal is finally over with, and they are celebrating. During the rehearsal, Kit's fountain had threatened to malfunction. Wheeled out-of-doors, prone and peevish, Eugene had challenged Vernon's vision one too many times, so that she had stopped the forward motion of the play to address, at length, each one of his complaints. Neve, the dog, had ambled onstage to urinate solemnly on a plaster of Paris statue. Laura Pasolini, second violinist, had arrived so late, the other three musicians had been forced to hum her solo section, and the black-and-white pony, Mr. Horse, meant to bear Carlo Gozzi to the front of

the audience to introduce the play, had balked and refused
to budge from an opening in the hedge they had specially
cut for it until Kit thought to proffer a lump of sugar, which
induced the pony to jolt forward as planned. Each time Vernon despaired, yanking on her cravat as if to strangle herself,
someone invariably repeated what another person had said
moments before: "Don't concern yourself, Vernon, it's for the
peasant children. It's for fun! They are children, not critics,
and will adore whatever we do!" So the comedy of rehearsal
errors had lurched on, taking twice as long as intended
because of delays, because of Eugene's objections, the pony's
balking, the dog's pissing, Pasolini's lateness, Kit's malfunc-
tioning waterworks, et cetera. By the time the assembled
party—Nerina and Flavia (who had translated Gozzi's Venetian dialect into comprehensible Tuscan), Eugene, Rezia, Ida,
Pia, Valentina, Countess Ludolf-Fabri (who had designed
the scenery with such artistry), Countesses Rasponi, and
Pasolini—finally sinks down, famished, to their candlit dinner, they share what Kit calls "the godliness of collaborators."
"Conspirators," Eugene amends. "We are promulgating illu-
sions for poor children, giving them candy instead of bread."
"Untrue!" Countess Ludolf-Fabri objects. "We are—what is
your English word?—'promulgating' magic for the children!
And who is to say that magic, fantasy, outrageous humor—
Gozzi's *L'Augellino*—is only for children, rich or poor? Isn't
magic for everyone?"

As Fortunata and her husband, Beppe, emerge from
the kitchen and cross the lawn bearing platters of cut pota-
toes roasted in olive oil, Florentine steaks, long green stalks
of favoli beans, a half wheel of Parmesan, loaves of bread,

bowls of cherries, a platter of cut quince with Vernon's own *uva fragole*, and an almond cake drenched in rum, Vernon cannot, in the midst of this feast, resist an improvisatory lecture on the history of Venetian commedia dell'arte, on the rivalry between its two greatest playwrights, Gozzi and Goldoni, each of whom asked a similar question: Is theater the right place for moral edification? With its potential for pontification and a too-boring lifelike representation—two crimes Gozzi accused Goldoni of—and with its equally dangerous inclination to fairy tale, magic, slapstick, bawdiness, and pandering to the audience's lowest appetites— felonies Goldoni, in turn, accused Gozzi of—what, then, was the highest responsibility, the social and philosophic purpose of theater?

"If one considers theater a projection of philosophy, an aesthetic form literally *acting out* a specific ethos or theologic stance, then we can see how thoroughly Goldoni and Gozzi oppose each other. Contemporaries, both wildly popular, Gozzi outside of Italy, Goldoni inside Italy, particularly Venice, where in one year alone . . ."

Cravat loosened, waistcoat flapping, Vernon drones on. Her half listeners, the Pasolinis, the Rasponis, the Cecchis, all the others, drowsy now with local wine, excellent food, and their host's opalescent powers of speech, drop into a soporific quiet, marked only by half-stifled yawns. Kit's seat is vacant; she has slipped off to check on her singing fountain, and Neve, slinking out from under the table, has loped off after her. Captivated by her own torrent of thoughts, marred only by a single violent hiccup, Vernon rambles on.

". . . Gozzi's plays, most profoundly, address transformation. Man to woman, woman to man, man to bird, old woman to tortoise . . . transformation reflecting, I put forth, what the Germans refer to as *Sehnsucht*, that longing or yearning that can never be satisfied, that desire to be released from fixed but impermanent form, so nearly supernatural in its . . ."

Eventually, even Vernon trails off, as a sleepy, affable silence settles over the assembled party. Countess Pasolini hums a little tune, *lucciole* (fireflies) wink in the nearby bay hedges, and, in the distance, they can hear the indistinct murmur of Kit's voice, her laughter. Sophia and Bella, neighbor girls, have run off to join Kit.

One of the violinists stands. She really must go home; it is getting late. There is mild joking as one by one, the friends rise to thank Vernon, confirm the time they should return for tomorrow's performance. Within minutes, the party has vanished, everyone gone back to their homes, as if the dinner, like the rehearsal, had been a dream, melting away, ephemeral, leaving only humble evidence—a table of soiled dishes, wineglasses, discarded napkins, a candelabra, its candles burned down to nothing now, still objects silent in the cypress and rose-scented darkness, awaiting dawn, when Fortunata and Beppe, now fast asleep in their bed, will emerge from the villa once more to act their parts and clear everything away.

"Kit. Everyone's gone home or to bed. What are you doing?"

"Bathing."

Vernon hesitates before lying down, stretching out in the grass beside Kit. "Stargazing?"

"No, bathing. Star bathing." Kit rolls onto her side, props herself on one elbow, her face close to Vernon's. "I am also a bit drunk. Pulcinella has gotten the best of me."

"Drunk? How amusing. You are such a surprise. Incapable, it seems, of boring me."

"Shhh." Kit puts one finger against Vernon's lips.

"But it's true. Everything you do amuses, intrigues—"

"Shhh, you really must be quiet now, dear V. I'm going to kiss you, a fact that, since I've just informed you of it, will no longer be a surprise."

"Don't. I can't."

"Why not? Didn't you write a note to me this morning?"

"I don't have it, won't ever have it."

"Have what? What are you talking about?"

"The gift you have. For inspiring love, giving love. Not in the sentimental sense, but really."

"Pif. Horse's ass." Kit leans in, kisses Vernon on the forehead, then in one lithe movement lies on top of her, full length, strokes her hair.

"Perfect V."

"I'm not."

"Yes, you are."

"I'm too horrid to be loved. Didn't I tell you I've been called hideous? Ugly?" Vernon hates the wet bit of self-pity leaking into her voice. "And I'm old."

Kit isn't listening. Instead, her kisses feather Vernon's face, the shadowy pool between her collarbones.

"You're not horrid or hideous or old. You're my angel, my dashing, witty, *très* delicate Gozzi."

This kiss is sudden, full on Vernon's lips, and smells of wine. She tries to relax, wills herself to unfreeze, and for a few incredible moments, she does. Sensations, all of them, melt her limbs—Kit's hand, slipping past the waistcoat and finding the way inside her shirt, rounding each of her breasts, slipping out, fingertips arrowing slow, sweet pressure down Vernon's stomach, resting with sureness between her legs, legs still wearing tight eighteenth-century breeches.

Panicked, Vernon sits up.

Kit rolls onto her back, hands loosely clasped behind her head. She acts as if nothing has happened. It's because she's a trainer of horses, Vernon thinks. She understands animal fear.

"I'm sorry, so sorry. I . . ."

Kit springs to her feet, as glad as if the world had just been handed to her. As indeed it has been.

"I did not hear, V., what you just said. Apologies are stupid." She reaches down a hand. Vernon grasps it and Kit lifts her, easily, to her feet.

"You're a ridiculously tiny person, V. *Une très petite femme.*" Pressing Vernon's hand to her lips, she turns to address an invisible audience: "*Regardez, Mademoiselle Violet est anglaise. Elle est ravissante et très cher a mon coeur. Ma Violet est un miracle! Et maintenant, chers amis, veuillez nous excuser car nous sommes très fatiguées. Bonne nuit à vous, à vous, à vous. . . . Bonne nuit à tous et que les dieux vous bénissent!*"

Kit wraps her arm around Vernon's waist, pulls her close. Crossing the silent garden to the house, Pulcinella and Gozzi giddily tiptoe up the stone stairs, trying not to wake anyone.

In the dark of her room, in the little space of her bed, Vernon's fingertips remember all the places Kit touched her. This is as much physical happiness as she can bear. She is sure of it.

V.

―――∞∞∞∞――――

At this moment in the seduction of Sylvia, that point of highest tension before the capitulation of the beloved to her lover, I am reminded of that most romantic of "white" ballets, Giselle, with its vapid score by Adolphe Adam and libretto by the French poet and abandonné, Théophile Gautier. Of that silly story of a beautiful peasant girl, Giselle, and a duke who disguises himself as a peasant so that he can court her, mixed in with the German folkloric tale of a secret glade, a hidden spot in the forest haunted by the Willis—ghosts of girls betrayed in love—spirits, gowned in white, who dance from midnight till dawn; any man unlucky enough to encounter the Willis is forced to dance with them to his death.

With Sylvia (forest creature!), we come near the end of my own version of Giselle, when a woman is lured, allured, deep into a hidden glade, not to die, but to dwell eternally, perhaps happily, with one ghost, one spirit.

I have always thought it would be incredibly dull, flagrantly dull, to be a chorus ballerina, dans le corps—a bit of white foam, sequined sparge, washing up, rolling back, the faint hissing of skirts and thumping of wood-blocked shoes, to *be a bit of vague, floating scenery behind the prima ballerina, the star. Not to be the principle dancer, not to be Giselle! (A fan of the art, I wrote Ballet of Nations, an antiwar piece that was a complete failure, only helping secure my disgrace as a pacifist among patriots and nationalists.)*

Ballets seldom tell happy stories. We reserve those for children, tales that are comedic, magical, and morally just. The stories Kit preferred. After the publication of our "Beauty and Ugliness," and the bad business with Berenson, all she wanted was to escape at the first excuse (Mrs. Head)—to hurry off to a sick friend's side as she once had rushed to mine.

I returned her to Palmerino by giving her a happy story, the play, and by giving her myself. For a time, these succeeded.

Industrious darling! Write without cessation, leave your bread and wine untouched. The most marvelous thing, the thing that tells me we are close to union now—she is telling it true, my story. Nearing the last pages, she writes faster, with all the oblivion of love. From time to time raises her head, pauses from her work, aware of me. Longing for me.

Ich liebe dich, mein Liebling, mein Engel. Come. Walk deep into Palmerino's garden, find the occult, green source of your name. Find those you have read about, gazed at in old photographs, half-written into existence.

Find me.

Sylvia

PHOTOGRAPHS. FANNED ACROSS her writing desk, pinned to the wall. For the hundredth time, she studies them, longing to break the code of images. Her handwriting, more Vernon's now, is illegible even to her. Pages of it, unnumbered, cross-written, disordered, scattered everywhere across the room. On the other desk, the one with her research books, all closed now, is a bit of dark chocolate, some stale *focaccia*, soured wine, a blackening pear. She stopped using her laptop days ago, no longer writing anything her agent would understand. If Sylvia had been methodical, too dull a writer before, she has disappeared into some freer direction now, recording only what she "hears" or "sees," whole scenes passing more rapidly than her fingers can fly. Page after page the gift comes, she is certain, from a female presence very near now, unseen, old, increasingly close.

L'Augellino Belverde

———— ◆◆◆◆ ————

LATE MORNING, AND THEY ARE DROWSY, languid with sleep, still in their patterned silk morning gowns. Kit has left hers unfastened, teasingly open. Raising Vernon's hand to her lips, she kisses each ink-stained finger, worshipfully, one by one. So close to yielding last night in the garden, Vernon has retreated into her habit of reserve this morning. Still, she does not remove her hand, allows the kisses, as if they were happening to someone else. Kit is patient. Leaning in, lightly stroking Vernon's arm. "A mask is seductive, *c'est vrai, chérie*? You smell of Madonna lilies, of little girls' dreams, *Vio letto ... petite V.*"

As Vernon shrinks back from her touch, Kit concentrates on spreading fresh butter over the top of one of Fortunata's delicious *cornetti*. Eats sensuously, indulgently, takes her time before speaking again.

"If a mask releases us from identity, frees us, this leads me to suppose we might all be acting falsely, dear V. A mask gives us liberty to unleash what is truest in us, most forbidden."

With an expression of surprise, Vernon claps down her delicate gilt-edged cup of coffee in its chipped gilt-edged saucer. "That is the most eloquent speech you have ever delivered before ten o'clock."

"Only because I am in love. Again."

She hands Pulcinella's black-ribboned bird mask to Vernon, who holds it before her eyes, gazes around the room. She feels different with her face hidden. Freer. Says so.

"That, V., is the entire allure of the actor's life." As she takes the mask back and ties it over her face, Kit's voice turns muffled, the black scimitar of paper beak waving about. Her mouth is still slightly full, savoring Fortunata's *cornetto* filled with apricot *marmellata* made from Palmerino's tiny but productive orchard. Standing up, she walks over to the window, turns to face Vernon, her voice distinct, clipped, vaguely Shakespearean.

"It appears this poor actor hath attempted to live a moral life, only to create scandal wherever she goes. . . . Isn't that fine, V.? I just invented it."

Occupied with powdering her peruke, her Gozzi wig, with a homemade mix of cornstarch, orris root, and wood ash, Vernon responds, her reply sarcastic, affectionate. "You are an absolute doyenne of the stage. You rival D'Annunzio's mistress, La Duse. Come here, kitten. What think you of my stinky wig? I've just doused it with a powder I had the chemist mix up for me yesterday."

Kit leaves her pose by the window, returns to the breakfast table. She reties the mask on Vernon, who, putting her whitened wig down before her on the table, submits to Kit's touch, uncharacteristically silent, docile. Standing close behind Vernon's chair, Kit slips both hands deep inside Vernon's dressing gown, caresses the bare, warm breasts, bends to kiss the back of Vernon's neck. "Tonight, *petite chérie?*"

"The play?"

"No, after. In your little garden. The garden only we know of. Come to me there."

Matilda, preceded by the citrus and bergamot scent of her crumpled lace handkerchief, marches in, ill-tempered, late for breakfast. Her flannel curl wrappers have come loose, dangling like small irritations off her gray-blond hair as she goes on about how Henry, shouting some nonsense about train schedules in his sleep, had kept her awake half the night.

Quietly refastening their robes, Kit and Vernon separate.

Overworked, dressed as an eighteenth-century servant— hardly different from the nineteenth-century servant she actually is—Fortunata hurries to open the street door each time the iron bell tinkles or the heavy brass door knocker raps against the freshly painted green door. She welcomes the *contadini*, reassures each solemn child clinging to its mother's skirts, gripping the hand of its father, older brother, or sister. As instructed, she leads families toward the strange, saturnine figure waiting nearby. At the sight of this figure, a few of the children burst into tears, hide behind their mothers, or whimper to be lifted up. The braver children simply stare. One boy, brash imp (the stamp of a revolutionary already on his cunning little face, the figure thinks, pleased), steps forward to poke whoever it is in the side.

The frightful figure is Count Gozzi, wearing the calf-length coat of gold brocade, lace cravat (cleaned that morning by Fortunata), waistcoat (stains removed by Fortunata), tight gold breeches, high black boots, and, atop the powdered peruke, a new item, a black felt tricorne hat. If the costume is outlandish, the face is fearsome. White with greasepaint, blotches of rouge fevering both cheeks, full, quivering lips similarly rouged and reddened to a bloody hue, eyebrows charcoaled into heavy, swooping wings, and eyes, rimmed in the same charcoal, looking down at each child—a myopic gaze, piercing, centuries old. Standing just inside the street door, in a dark part of the garden, Vernon must bend to peer close at the children, press her hands on their little shoulders, puff her breath, slightly rotten, in their faces.

Once they survive the old playwright, muttering to himself in some antique Venetian dialect (invented by Vernon), the children, with their families, continue up a narrow gravel path bordered by tall, regally stemmed white Madonna lilies. Orange paper lanterns, lit from within by candles, hang like round, glowing fruits in the lower branches of trees. Soon, they encounter a second figure, less fearsome than the first. With precise timing, just as each family approaches, Pulcinella leaps from behind an immense magnolia tree, claps her hands, and capers about in such a ridiculous fashion, the children laugh, forgetting fearsome old Count Gozzi, from whose decaying clutches they have just escaped. Dressed in flapping white pantaloons and a billowy white tunic, Pulcinella has concealed her face behind a bird's mask of stiff black paper, her head made twice as tall by the high white *coppolone*. Stopping in mid-caper, she bows, straightens up, and, from her pocket, ceremonially presents each child with a tin whistle, along with whispered instructions: "Only tootle on this whistle at the exact moment Pulcinella asks! There will be magic! But you must not pipe upon your magical instrument, not make one squeak till I ask, lest our poor actors and the dear fairies who help them be cast into a sad, dreadful, permanent sleep. Wait till I, Pulcinella, ask for your help!"

As paper lanterns throw exaggerated shadows over their small, bewildered faces, the children grip their tin whistles, in possession of some new, thrilling power. Kit had invented the idea of whistles to include the children, to give them each a little part. She had suggested it during last night's rehearsal, when Eugene, objecting to everything possible about the play, had interrupted her. "Speaking as the Devil's most humble advocate," he began, until Vernon, losing patience, cut him off and ordered him back to his room if he couldn't keep quiet. The others thought Kit's idea excellent, and early the next morning, one of the musicians set about procuring a quantity of cheap tin whistles.

The twenty or so children, clutching their whistles, a few giving them over to their parents for safekeeping, make their way up the gravel path, following Pulcinella's cheerful directions: "Go toward the music, darlings! Mozart's enchanting flute will bring you to a bend in the path. Follow the orange lanterns until you hear the plash of a fountain. Once there, two woodland fairies, Flora and Rosa, will be waiting to take you to your seats."

They move between the orange lanterns and fragrant white trumpets of lilies; the balmy summer air, the thick, dark trees arching overhead, and the not-too-distant music of Mozart all cast an intoxicating spell. Just as Pulcinella had promised, as they emerge from the path onto a large lawn with a splashing marble fountain at its center, two creatures float up in ballerina skirts of pink tulle, fairies, each with a garland of wild pink roses on her long, loose, dark hair. Gossamer wings undulate from their pale, bare shoulders as, with sweet-mingled voices, they invite the children to sit with their parents on long wooden benches. Off to one side of the smooth-cut lawn, near a weeping willow, four musicians in red-and-yellow-striped frock coats play, turning parchment pages of music set out on wooden stands, each with its brass sconce and lit candle. The benches upon which the children and their families sit face a stage scrolled and painted in gold. Kerosene lanterns illumine the front of the stage, while at either end, floor sconces hold candles, lit and blazing. The dark green velvet curtain is open; the stage's painted backdrop is a magnificent Caneletto-like scene of Venetian canals, gondolas, and grand palazzos. Rising behind this imaginary view of Venice is a black wall of Palmerino's cypress trees, stately and enigmatic.

Rosa and Flora vanish into an opening of large oak and magnolia trees, reappear holding small wicker baskets. "Here," they whisper, reaching into their baskets, placing something in each child's hand, gently closing tiny fingers over it. "Eat this, then make a wish." When the children open their fingers, they see a sparkling sugared violet. Placed upon the tongue, the flower dissolves into a sweet, lingering dream.

Once all the families are seated, waiting with restless expectation, Count Gozzi suddenly appears, riding out from between tall bay hedges astride a black-and-white pony, Mr. Horse. In front of the stage, he reins in his steed, turns to face the audience. Raising one hand, signaling the musicians to stop playing, he removes his tricorne hat with a flourish, bows from the waist. One child, remembering her earlier terror, erupts into wails and is carried off by her mother. In the subsequent quiet, Neve, locked into a cage-like enclosure and unaccustomed to confinement, sends up a piteous howl.

Count Gozzi dismounts, and Beppe leads Mr. Horse away as the playwright strides back and forth, heartily welcoming everyone to his finest play, *L'Augellino Belverde*. Under the cover of his speech, the actors tiptoe up the short flight of stairs, assume their places behind the now-closed green curtain. His little introduction finished, the old playwright, too, slips behind the curtain as Mozart's Prelude and Fugue no. 5 begins. Eugene, to one side of the stage, clumsily costumed as a marble statue, draws open the curtain, revealing the scene of a piazza in daytime, somewhere in Venice. . . .

Unable to make sense of the fast-paced plot, the children still know whom they like and dislike, who is good and who is bad, as, wide-eyed, they follow the actors' silly speeches and slapstick antics. Each scene, more fantastic than the last, culminates in the appearance of a magical green bird, *l'augellino belverde,* swooping down from a low branch on a real tree close to the stage, the audience knowing the bird is a prince under a wicked spell, in love with the pretty girl. If even the children's parents can scarcely follow the frantic twists and nonsense turns of the play, the fathers appreciate the sly references to *"l'uccello,"* slang for penis, how it darts and flits around the pretty girl.

And if Carlo Gozzi's philosophic message, as Vernon had droned on about it the night before, is utterly lost, what does it matter? The magical effects of a play performed out-doors in a candle- and lantern-lit garden are enough—the mock sword fighting, boisterous singing and kissing, the large, fabulous green bird zooming back and forth above the stage. And then comes the moment Pulcinella had promised—when she leaps onstage, white *coppolone* bob-bling, and begs them to blow hard upon their whistles; they must help her to break, once and for all, the wicked spell cast upon the poor prince! As the children tootle and wheeze upon their tin whistles, filled with an almost desper-ate complicity of faith, the fountain of white marble, silent throughout the play, sends jets of water sparkling up into the night, striking each of the glass apples dangling from the topmost marble basin, so they do indeed "sing." The effect is fantastic, the prince so perfectly saved, the spell so boldly broken, even the adults burst into wild applause and shouts of "Bravo, bravo," until the play ends with Eugene, as monument, yanking the curtain closed. He has to open and close it three more times as the actors, holding hands, bow together, and the applause goes on with endless cries of "Bravo, bravo!" As the waves of clapping diminish, one child can be heard sobbing with overexcitement as several others race from their seats and climb onstage to shake hands with the characters, especially the pretty girl and the old witch, pulling on them to see if they are real. While the green bird flaps back and forth above the stage, chased by several older boys, in the garden, another child, climbing up to "pick" one of the singing apples, topples into the fountain and has to be carried into the house to be dried off by Fortunata. The gossamer fairies, net wings drooping, dart out from behind the stage, where they had managed all the props, to take charge of a table set up beforehand with platters of honey and anise cookies and a punch bowl of iced lemonade, a scatter of purple violets carpeting its surface. The four musicians play Hayden as, just behind them, hundreds of *lucciole* wink bits of fire among the green tendrils of willow.

Sated by the entertainment, dessert, and the late hour, families begin to say good-bye, gathering up children, drifting down garden paths they had walked up earlier. Mothers and fathers, tired and silent, think of work awaiting them tomorrow. A few of the children are giddy, silly, others half-sick with excitement; some yawn sleepily. One child can be heard retching miserably into a clump of peony bushes.

Soon, all of the families will have have vanished out the gate, gone down the road in one direction or the other, most on foot, a few with mule-drawn carts to carry them. An hour or so later, the actors, musicians, even the fairies, Rosa and Flora, all content with the evening's success, have gone home, too.

Rubbing the small, itchy rash on her forehead, caused by the powdered wig she has just tugged off, Vernon sinks down at the table beneath the pergola to savor the evaporating world of her creation. On the empty stage, dried gouts of wax river down the tall sides of the floor sconces, their flames long ago gone out. Kerosene has burned off in half the lamps; low flames in the others gutter out. Eighteenth-century Venice returns to darkness. Several of Kit's hand-painted theater programs litter the grass around her feet. Vernon finishes off a glass of punch, tries one of the anise cookies. The perfume from Kit's Scottish roses, whitely massed and gleaming just above her, is intoxicating. From a cypress tree nearby, a nightingale sings, and its mate softly answers, while within the clipped bay hedges, a glittering net of *lucciole* winks with fainter and fainter light before going completely dark.

"Buonasera, Signore Gozzi. I guessed you would not look for me, so I instead have found you. Come!"

Oh, she cannot. "Where?"

"For a walk, V. Only a walk. It's too early to go inside. I'm wide awake after such a triumph. Come, you must celebrate—it was splendid, our play."

A walk. Nothing else? Just so she doesn't have to feel, or, worse, fail to feel.

They walk, only the sound of their feet moving over gravel, down a path, through leaves.

"You are like a somnambulist, darling." Kit lifts up some heavy vines. A veil.

Vernon hesitates.

"*Une surprise, chérie.*"

In the clearing, soft blankets, a place to lie down.

"That's right," Kit says.

Standing near Vernon, she unties and draws off her poet's shirt, the costume she wore as Pulcinella, figure of melancholy. Undoes the drawstring of her loose white pants, lets them fall to the grass. Kneeling before Vernon, she unfastens each button of Count Gozzi's stained, lace-cuffed shirt, slides it slowly down over the pale shoulders, stops at Vernon's small pink-tipped breasts. Looks up. "Exquisite, darling girl."

So Violet escapes the one who talked, ruled, wounded with words, struck out, kept love far away for so long. Irrelevant, she doesn't know how or what, exactly, to do. At last, it doesn't matter, the cost to her frightened, walled-off Vernon self; she yields.

Il Morte

How I adored the music of the seventeenth and eighteenth centuries—Handel, Bach, Gluck, Frescobaldi, Boccherini, Provenzale, Caccini, Monteverdi, Carissimi, Scarlatti the elder, Mozart . . . Herr Mozart! Said to have kept a finch in a cage, composing a concerto entirely by mimicking its song. The small yellow finch, thistle eater, harbinger of Christ's sufferings, there in Raphael's Madonna of the Goldfinch, in Barocci's Holy Family, others. My first book, a study of eighteenth-century Italian music, written when I was twenty-four. So young. My last book, three years ago, a study of the emotional and imaginative effects of music. Too fagged, stupefied by little heart attacks, to write anymore. Visitors are burdensome, though I am fond of Dr. Sexton, who looks in on me weekly. That woman won my affection after I complained to her about my ugliness, and she replied, "Perhaps, but yours is a baroque ugliness, softened by wit, the charm of intelligence." A baroque ugliness. How I approve of that!

Music surpasses the noise of human conversation. The first poem a prayer, the first prayer a song, the first song a slight breath . . . the whole world, would we listen, imparadised by *sound. My deafness shuts me deep inside myself. Infurled into vastation, a destruction called silence. I, who fattened on talk, feasted on the sound of myself, used speech to defend my timidity, my shame at being pitied, stared at, whispered about: ugly child, ugly girl, hideous, unsexed creature! I became one sound: <u>Vernon Lee</u>. A solitary charisma wearing a man's name, in male dress, with masculine speech. Hours of erudition and wit flowing forth in French, Italian, German, English, whatever tongue I chose. Now, I live caged in the thickest of quiets. I still possess "le chant interieur," the memory of music, but memory wanders frail now, with small sense or reason.*

As memory goes, so the heart, the physical, feeling heart.

Kit left me a second time for Mrs. Head. After I went to her, hearing she was so ill, she died in my arms on July 8, 1921. Of the things still in our hearts, we neither spoke nor said a word. Others died in letters, the cessation of letters from this person or that.

A general seediness, a roaring in my ears, pen, ink, books—I still sometimes scribble in margins, agreeing with, arguing for, the old beauty of intermingled thoughts.

Was all my work a failure? Most of it has vanished, even if it made the slightest impression.

Was my life of momentary importance, followed by obliteration?

Our conscience grows quieter.

Unable to hear the scrape of my chair as I push myself back, or the sound of my favorite pen, dropping off my writing desk to the floor, I am called to the moon, full, icy, and brilliant in the eastern sky, to the old spires of cypress and quarry rock, black frieze behind the moon's sailing curve. I step onto the balcony, rest my hands on its railing, sing the deep joy of Ben Jonson's hymn to Diana, virgin goddess of the moon.

> *Queen and huntress, chaste and fair,*
> *Now the sun is laid to sleep,*

"Fortunata, stop what you are doing! Work is endless. Look up! This is all we have."

> *Seated in thy silver chair . . .*

Is it preferable to die alone, of beauty?

Little Violet Paget, so grave and solitary a girl with her books, her grim green glasses—dear child. So much she had hoped for in music, fable, fairy tale, in theater, poetry, love— we leave that now for a more ethereal sound, divine sound that only faintly, if ever, reaches earth.

The pain, when it comes, is brief. Life, as she had known it, a dream.

Sylvia

————◁≫▷————

SHE HEARS NATALIA'S GUESTS BEGIN to arrive, to greet one another. Some go inside; most remain on the flagstone patio, talking, sitting at the cloth-covered table, candles lit and glowing down its length. The sky is starless, black.

From behind the shutters, Sylvia, in her green silk gown, looks down, recognizes a few of the guests. Natalia and her husband. The astronomer in his frayed pink shirt. Countess Baldini from the Mass at San Martino. The others she does not know. Then Remo. Wearing long pants, a rumpled white shirt, and the old-fashioned dress shoes she had last seen tucked beneath a chair in the laundry shed, he carries food out from the kitchen, setting it down along the table. Large platters and bowls of food, plates, baskets, wine from Palmerino's grapes decanted in dark green bottles with rough-woven straw coverings, smaller versions of the enormous glass bottles she had seen piled outside the shed. Everyone sits, eats, conversing in the easy manner of people who know one another and are largely content. Richard Asquith is the exception. With his head bowed low to his plate, the astronomer eats with fierce, solitary

concentration. Conversations are in Italian; Sylvia understands almost nothing. Perhaps she should dress, go downstairs. She has been invited. During their visit last summer,
Natalia mentioned to Philip and Sylvia an odd thing she
had noticed. Over the years, certain people who came to
Villa il Palmerino admitted feeling "called" there, and if one
cared to get metaphysical about it, a few confessed to some
sense of destiny, even fate. "I never advertise my rentals,"
Natalia said. "People simply appear."

Someone taps on his wineglass. Eventually, unevenly,
the guests fall silent. A man stands, offers a toast to his wife.
Tomorrow, he says, is her birthday. Everyone raises a glass,
drinks to the wife, who makes a modest joke. Conversation,
laughter resume. The table, the food and wine, ten or twelve
friends seated beneath a vine-covered pergola on a perfect
summer's night—Sylvia looks down on this scene as if it
were a photograph, one photograph superimposed over a
second, older image, gazing until the faces merge, blur, star-
tle. She feels as if these guests, even herself, upstairs, concealed from view, have come home. Candlelight smudges
each of their faces, plays tricks, confuses, reshapes features.

At that moment, hearing her name, she understands
who is calling her.

Remo limps out from the kitchen, carrying a platter of
uncooked fava beans with sliced white cheese. Sylvia, barefoot, waits in the shadow of the staircase until he is outside
with the others. Slipping into the kitchen, she opens the
back door and begins to run (so soon out of breath, a slight
pain in her chest) past the lawn, vineyard, vegetable garden, orchard. Finds the overgrown footpath where she had

guessed, always known, it was. The pain in her chest a cleaving light. Parting the silver veil of vines, Sylvia steps into a moonlit glade, kept secret by a wall of cool, dead cyprus. All that is left is to stand, scarcely breathing, and await the great female soul that is Palmerino to reveal herself and take her.

Early on the morning of June 29, Giustina Alberini's caretaker discovers the body of an American writer, Sylvia Casey, in a small clearing not far from the laundry shed where he had gone to dress for the day's work. A coroner will later rule Ms. Casey's death the result of an undiagnosed heart condition. Her few belongings, including a book she had been working on, will be packed up and mailed to her ex-husband. At his request, the body will be cremated, the ashes interred in a new, seldom visited section of Allori Cemetery.

When Sylvia's agent, who had decided not to retire, receives the unfinished, unreadable manuscript, he has no idea what to do with it. Eventually, he sends it out to be bound. On the day it is returned to his office, he observes that it lacks a title. Before placing it on a high shelf beside Sylvia Casey's published books, he takes a pencil and, late for a business lunch, scrawls across the pale green cover *Palmerino.*

Acknowledgments

With thanks to my friend Giuditta Viceconte, for introducing me to the magic of Federica Parretti, Stefano Vincieri, and Villa il Palmerino. Thanks, too, to Giuliano Angeli for offering his personal tour of Vernon Lee's villa and gardens, and to Beatrice Angeli for providing true sanctuary. To Mario and Millie Materassi, cherished friends, for welcoming me to Florence years ago and to their daughter, Luisa, for timely assistance with my Italian. To Susanna Casprini and Simona Lumachelli, for supporting my earliest ideas for this novel, and to Gyorgyi Szabo in Paris and Jillian Robinson in Tucson, for reading drafts in progress.

I am indebted to Colby College, Waterville, Maine, Special Collections, and the Gabinetto Vieusseux. I wish to offer particular thanks to Alyson Price, archivist at the British Institute. I am grateful to the Bogliasco Foundation, especially Melissa Phegley, and the Bogliasco Study Center, Liguria, Italy, especially Ivana Folle, director, and Alessandra Natale, associate director. Deep thanks as well to the Ledig-Rowohlt Foundation and Château de Lavigny, especially Sophie Kandaouroff, manager, Jens-Martin Eriksen, and their daughter, Tatiana.

Great thanks to my agent, Joy Harris, my visionary publisher, Erika Goldman, and her remarkable Bellevue Literary Press family, Leslie Hodgkins, Lissa Rivera, Adam Beaudoin, Molly Mikolowski, Carol Edwards, and Anne McPeak.

Special thanks to Father Murray Bodo, OFM, spiritual mentor, poet, and friend.

And to my daughters, Noelle Pritchard Barkley and Caitlin Pritchard Rushing, and my Sudanese son, William Akoi Mawwin. I am blessed by their love and support.

Lastly, I would be remiss if I did not extend thanks to Simon, dachshund extraordinaire and determined muse.

Grazie a tutti.

BELLEVUE LITERARY PRESS has been publishing
prize-winning books since 2007 and is the first and only
nonprofit press dedicated to literary fiction and nonfiction
at the intersection of the arts and sciences. We believe
that science and literature are natural companions for
understanding the human experience. Our ultimate goal is
to promote science literacy in unaccustomed ways and offer
new tools for thinking about our world.
To support our press and its mission, and for our full
catalogue of published titles, please visit us at blpress.org.

BELLEVUE LITERARY PRESS
New York